THE WARNING

"I am sad," said Silver calmly to Lorens. "But if you don't put down that gun, I shall have to shoot you through the head."

In silence, Lorens' hand jerked down inch by inch until the gun lay on the floor.

"Now stand up, señor," said Silver. "Forgive me—but if you make one quick move, my poor thumb on the hammer of this gun will be frightened, and the hammer will fall, and you will go up to join the sky people."

Lorens obeyed Silver's instructions, panting, silent. "What a cursed fool I was! Tonight I argued on your side of the fence. But I'll tell you, I'll find a way to come back to you. How you'll pray to die—how you'll beg for hell itself when my hands get to work on you, one day."

Books by Max Brand

Published by POCKET BOOKS

Max Brand

THE MAN FROM MUSTANG

A KANGAROO BOOK
PUBLISHED BY POCKET BOOKS NEW YORK

POCKET BOOKS, a Simon & Schuster division of
GULF & WESTERN CORPORATION
1230 Avenue of the Americas, New York, N.Y. 10020

ISBN: 0-671-81757-4

First Pocket Books printing June, 1978

Trademarks registered in the United States and other countries.

Printed in the U.S.A.

THE MAN FROM MUSTANG

Chapter I

THE PRAIRIE FIRE

ON the brow of the last hill that spilled from the knees of the mountains toward the prairie, under the last tree, "Silver" sat with his knees hugged in his arms and watched the rider in the distance, and the prairie fire behind him.

Parade, with bridle off and saddle on, grazed near by, biting off the short, sweet grass close to the roots, eating greedily, as though he knew that the taste of this pasturage was much sweeter than the tall, dry grasses beneath him. Now and then he jerked up his head and looked suddenly at his master, and then all about him, with pricking ears, for he understood perfectly that to the wolfish keenness of his scent and to his quickness of ear and eye, Silver looked for warning if any danger came his way. Parade was a combination of stallion and sentinel, the guardian and the servant of the man.

The day was hot and dry. Silver had taken off the big sombrero as he sat in the shade, and thereby exposed the two marks of gray hair above his temples that looked like incipient horns sprouting, and had given him his universal nickname of "Silvertip." Now he made himself at ease. He had been long enough in the mountain wilderness which he loved, and it seemed to him a typical irony of fate that as he turned his face back toward the dwellings of man he should see a rider on the plain and a grass fire at the same time. For among men there was always danger.

The fellow who jogged his horse quietly along seemed unaware of the coming of the fire for a long time. It had begun as a small point, like a dust cloud,

7

rolling. It increased. Evidently a wind was favoring it, and finally a gust of that breeze went whispering through the leaves above the head of Silver.

By this time the grass fire had gathered both speed and frontage, and was leaving behind it a widening wedge of black against the pallor of the prairie grass. At the same moment the lone rider became aware of the danger behind him. Silver laughed to see the man bring his mustang to a gallop and flatten out along the neck of the horse.

It was high time, but time enough, for the horse could move a great deal faster than the fire itself, though that was now galloping like a thousand wild beasts, wallowing, plunging, throwing forward a leaning wall of smoke, as though a dense mass of skirmishers were running forward with rifles firing constantly. Fast as the wind blew, pressing the smoke forward, the speeding flames ran almost as quickly. Now they rushed down a hollow with a slower gait. Now they leaped up a slope, and at the crest hurled upward a gigantic cloud of fire, as though in excess of strength. A god seemed to be rioting in that flame, bounding between earth and heaven, trailing his cloak of smoke high up in the sky.

The fugitive, in the meantime, was gaining rapidly on the wall of danger, when all at once, as he came close enough for Silver to make out that the horse was small and the man big, the mustang went down and hurled its rider far away, spinning head over heels.

The horse tried to rise at once, but a dangling foreleg prevented it. The man, on the other hand, lay perfectly still, face down, twisted as though his body had been broken in the middle.

Silver had the bridle on Parade almost before he had finished noting these things. For both horse and man lay directly in the path of the fire.

With the throatlatch unfastened, he sprang into the saddle. The big golden chestnut got under way like a frightened deer. Down the hillside he streaked, across the green like a meteor down the blue arch of the sky, and struck the level, where the tall prairie grasses whipped like splashing water about his shoulders. That impediment could not slow his speed or shorten his stride.

And angling straight toward the danger point, Silver rode him between the fallen horse and the fallen rider.

It would be a near thing. Already the running flame put out an arm of crimson and smoke that enveloped the struggling horse. The poor beast screamed with agony. Silver, twisting in the saddle, put a bullet through its head from his revolver.

Right behind him came the sweeping fire. The wind that hurried above the flames dropped a shower of sparks and whole bunches of burning grass that seemed to have been uprooted by the force of the draft! And little new fires caught hold on the dryness of the grass even before the main body of the flame had rolled to them.

One of these spots of fire was spreading at the side of the fallen rider as Silver came up. He called out. Parade stood on braced feet, and Silver, without dismounting, leaned far down from the saddle.

He took that burden under the armpits and hauled it up. The head fell back as though on a broken neck, to show Silver a young, brown face, almost absurdly homely. There was enough nose and jaw for two ordinary men, yet what the face enjoyed in length it lacked in width. But the forehead was good, and what Silver saw first and last was the frown that lingered on the brow. A dead man's face would have been smooth, he told himself, but there was the promise of life!

With that limp body in his arms, he called again; and Parade went like a flashing gesture through the tall grass, back to the shorter growth on the hillside.

There Silver deposited his burden. He had to spend a minute beating out sparks that had begun to ignite his clothes. Parade was dancing because of a smoking place on his mane. When that was out, there were more burning spots on the clothes of the stranger.

In the meantime, the roar of the prairie fire went by,

leaving acres of glowing red behind it, and the black, smoking heap where the mustang lay dead.

The unconscious man now stirred suddenly, and sat up with a gasp. He said nothing for some time. First his eye marked the distant rush and roar of the conflagration. Then he looked down and actually patted the short green of the grass on which he was sitting. At last he marked the place where the dead horse lay.

At that he started to his feet with an exclamation. It seemed to Silver that he was about to run down into the grass toward the dead horse, though there were still flaming bits that far behind the head of the fire. Silver caught his shoulder and held him.

"You'll burn your boots, and spoiled leather won't help that dead horse," said Silver.

"No, you're right," said the other slowly. He looked at Silver with a dull eye of suffering. "He's eaten enough right out of my hand," said he. "And now the fire's eaten him—right off the ground."

He smiled. His whole face twisted with grief that he fought again.

"He was a good-looking horse," said Silver gently.

"He was a right good one. He was a cutting horse," said the stranger, wiping his hands on his leather chaps absently. "You put him on the tail of a calf and he'd follow that calf to kingdom come. Yes, sir, and head it off before ever it got there, in spite of anything. That's the kind of a cutting horse he was. But the fire got him—fire!" He shuddered as he said it.

"I put a bullet through his head just before the fire ate him," said Silver.

The stranger looked Silver up and down, but saw no gun. A gleaming gesture made a big Colt with three extra inches of barrel on it appear from beneath the coat of Silver and disappear again.

"I'm thankin' you," said the stranger. "And you didn't have no lot of time on your hands, neither."

He looked down at the spots on his own clothes, some of which were still faintly smoking. Then he eyed the damaged costume of Silver. Suddenly he grinned.

"I'm goin' to be owin' you a suit of clothes in exchange for the skin that I'm still wearing," he said.

"All right," answered Silver.

"Poor old Jerry!" said the man under his breath. "I'll tell you what he was," he added suddenly. "He was a partner. You know?"

"I know," said Silver.

The stranger glanced toward Parade.

"Yeah, you know, all right," he agreed. "Maybe you know even a lot better'n I do. When I was camping out, he'd watch over me at night like a dog. We've been on desert marches when he ate half of my bacon and drank sugar and milk. We been on marches when I've boiled his oats and halved 'em with him. Jerry," concluded the stranger with a broad sweep of his hand, "was a horse!"

"He was," said Silver. "Right up to the end, he was trying to get to you and tell you that the fire was coming."

"What happened?" asked the man.

"He put his foot in a hole in the ground, I guess," said Silver. "He broke his leg when he fell, and he couldn't get up."

The stranger took off his sombrero and wiped from his face sweat that was never produced by the heat of the sun. He swallowed hard. Then suddenly he faced Silver.

"I don't know your name," he said. "Mine is Ned Kenyon."

Silver took the hand.

"People call me Jim," he said, "or Arizona Jim, or Arizona. I don't care much what I'm called."

A slight shadow passed over the face of Kenyon, but it was gone at once.

"Any name is the right name," he said, "for me to tell you that I've had my hide saved by you. The day before my wedding day, too!"

He grinned broadly, and the ugliness disappeared from his face, it was so lighted.

"The luck stays with a plumb happy man," said Kenyon.

"It does," agreed Silver.

"Look," said the stranger impulsively. "I want you to see her right away. I want that you should know you've done more than save my hide; because maybe you've kept a lot finer person than me from trouble. I want you to see her."

He jerked a flat leather case from his inside coat pocket, and then paused, and his blue, small eyes lingered wistfully on the handsome face of Silver, as though asking for permission.

"I want to see it," said Silver. "Let's have a look."

That was enough.

Ned Kenyon opened the leather case and displayed the picture.

"It don't do her justice," he said, sidling around to Silver. "But you just get a sort of general idea, is all."

A small, stinging shock had passed into the brain of Silver as he looked. A queer numbness spread in his mind. For as he stared, he told himself that there was only one thing under heaven he could be sure of, and that was that such a girl as this could never marry Ned Kenyon.

Silver saw her in profile, but he could tell the bigness and the straightness of the eyes, and the refinement of the mouth, and the proud lift of the chin. A king could have married her proudly, and not for her beauty only, but for things of mind and spirit that spoke out of her face.

Half squinting, Silver called up the image of the man beside him, the long, gaunt body, the long, gaunt face.

No, he decided, the thing could not be. Perhaps the poor fellow had this mania—that being unattractive to most women, he had picked up the portrait of some reigning beauty of New York or Paris, and carried it about with him, to boast pathetically of his triumph.

"She's very beautiful," said Silver gravely, giving back the picture.

Kenyon took it in both hands and shook his head.

"It ain't the beauty that counts. It's the heart underneath it," he said. "She's a clean-bred one. Oh, she's as straight as a string, let me tell you!"

"I'll put my money that she is," said Silver.

"Brave, and honest, and sort of simple and quiet, and about perfect," said Kenyon slowly.

He put the picture back inside his coat.

"To-morrow at noon," said he, "we're going to be married in Mustang. And I wish that you were going to be there, partner. That's what I wish. That you were going to be there, so that she could thank you face to face. I'd like to have you hear her voice—just once. Because it's the sort of a thing that you'd never forget if you lived for a hundred years."

Silver looked at the vanishing smoke of the prairie fire, far away, for it had been running like wild horses all this time, cleaving a greater and greater wedge of black through the pale prairie grass.

The thing could not be. Every instinct in him spoke against it. She could not, being what she was, marry this lean grotesque of a cow-puncher.

"How far is Mustang?" he asked.

"Only twenty miles!" said the other eagerly.

"Then I'll go there with you," said Silver. "It's a long time since I've seen a wedding."

Chapter II

THE SIMPLE MAN

THERE was no doubt of one thing—that just as firmly as Silver was convinced that the wedding would never take place, just so firmly was Ned Kenyon assured that on the morrow he would be the happiest man in the world, and that this girl would be his wife.

He was ready to talk of her. Words about her overflowed his lips.

She was only twenty. Her name was Edith Alton. All the perfections that God could give to a woman had been showered upon her.

Perhaps, thought Silver, it might be an old acquaintance, one of those deep affections that grow up from years spent together—as, for instance, Kenyon might have been for long the foreman on her father's ranch. Or perhaps there were hidden qualities in this man—he might be, for all his rather ungrammatical language, an artist, an inspired poet, or a philosopher such as Silver had met in the West more than once, filled with wisdom that seems to rise like sap from the ground.

"You've known her a long time?" asked Silver.

"Seven days!" said Kenyon.

Again the numb incredulity spread through the brain of Silver. Seven days!

"That's not long," remarked Silver. "Love at first sight, I suppose?"

"No," answered Kenyon. "Not for her. For me, yes. But not for her. I saw her at the railroad, and I drove the stage that brought her up to Mustang. I hardly kept the wheels on the road, because I was turning all the time to look at her. And then the next day was my day off the driver's seat, and I went to a dance, and there she turned up, and I danced with her, part of a dance.

"But she wanted to talk more than to dance. And she asked me to take her outside. We walked up and down under the pine trees, into the black of the trees, and out into the white of the moon. Mostly talking. Mostly me talking. And she listening, with her head a little on one side. It's dead easy to talk to a girl like that!" he exclaimed. "And there was me, that never had found a girl in the world that would pay no attention to me! And there was me, with the queen of the world, as you might say!"

Silver, as he walked along at the side of his companion, the stallion following without the need of a lead, sighed a little. The problem was beginning to grow more and more unfathomable to him. Behind it there lay a mystery as profound as a pit, a darkness which his eye could not penetrate. But with every step he made at the side of this man, the more convinced he became of the man's steel-true honesty and worth. There was not a crooked bone in his body, not a shadowy thought in his brain.

"You talked of a lot of things?" asked Silver.

"We talked about me," said the stage driver. "She seemed a lot interested in that. I told her about being a kid on the farm in Dakota, and about the way the winter lasted, and the way the spring came up, and the way the snow first melted, and the spring skating, and a lot of things like that, and how I came farther west, and about prospecting, and all that, and how I started to drive the stage, and got along at that because I got a way with horses. And she listened like a baby to music all the time, with her head a little over on one side, and now and then turning her head, and smiling at me a bit. In a way," said Kenyon, "that I couldn't tell you about it. Just a kind of a smile that soaked into you, like spring sunshine!"

He was no poet, either, thought Silver—just a fine,

honest, decent fellow, with unprobed virtues of courage and decency. But a mate for that girl in the picture, with her lifted chin and her straight-looking eyes, and the sensitive nose and lips?

No! Whatever happened, it could not be that she intended to marry Ned Kenyon.

"You go on and ride," Kenyon was saying. "I don't mind walking. I'm pretty good at it. And with Edith to talk about, I could walk to the end of the world."

Something jerked at Silver, something pulled him up in revolt even to hear Ned Kenyon call the girl by her first name—and yet he was to marry her on the morrow!

"If you could ride half the time while I walked," said Silver, "it would be all right. But this horse doesn't like most people, and he'd be fighting every minute to get you out of the saddle."

"Would he?" murmured Kenyon.

He gave the brim of his hat a jerk.

"I ain't boasting," he said, "but the fact is that I'm pretty fair with horses my own self. I'd like to try him, if you don't mind, stallion or no stallion!"

"Would you?" said Silver, smiling. Then he laid a hand on Kenyon's bony shoulder and added: "Don't do it. He's a trickster. He knows a thousand ways of getting a man out of the saddle, and the worst of him is that when the rider drops, he has a way of trying to savage the unlucky fellow. I'd be on hand, but I might not be close enough to call him off in time. I don't doubt that you're a good rider—but I'd rather not have you try him."

Ned Kenyon looked wistfully at the golden stallion, and then he sighed.

"You know your own self and your own horse better than anybody else," he observed. "And it's the seeing of a man like you, Arizona, with a horse like that, that makes me wonder how Edith can look at me once and want to look at me twice. But I remember folks saying years ago that the likes of men for women and women for men there's no accounting for. Only, when I think of you, riding on a horse like that—well, I can't help thinking that Edith may shake her head a coupla times. Only I know that there's nothing in her but faith. For what would the world amount to, Arizona, if there was anything behind a face and an eye and a voice like hers except truth and honesty, and the kind of love that won't die in a long winter?"

Silver, listening to this speech, which was drawled out with a good many pauses, while Ned Kenyon found proper words to express himself, looked several times down to the ground, and several times with his narrowed eyes peered into the horizon like a hawk.

He said at last: "A man or a woman that lied to you, Ned, would need a hanging; and I'd be glad to pull on the rope!"

"Would you, Arizona?" asked the simple man. "I think you mean it, too. I think it's been a great day for me, Arizona. Because, look here—a man can't live by a woman only, but he needs a friend, too. And I don't know that I've ever had a real friend in all my born days."

"Never a friend?" asked Silver, starting. "Do you mean that, Kenyon? Do you mean that you've seen through the lot and found them all a worthless gang?"

"Looked through them?" echoed Kenyon. "Man, man, who am I to be looking through folks? No, no! There's three out of four or four out of five that I would be glad enough to have as friends. I'm no one to make big pretendings. Any right man is a good man for me to talk to and keep to. It's not my choosing, but the choice of the other people, that doesn't fall on me. Unless they want to cheat me out of money, or talk kind to me to-day just in order to make a fool of me to-morrow. And so it's come about that I've never had a friend in my life, until to-day it sort of looks as though *you* might be a friend to me, Arizona!"

He slowed his step and turned his frank, open eye on Silvertip; and the heart of Silver swelled in him.

He put his hand again on the thin shoulder of Kenyon and said carefully, weighing his words: "I've had few friends, too. And most of those I've had are behind me somewhere." He made a gesture, as though dropping something over his shoulder. Then he went on: "But I think that you and I could pull together as long as we're traveling in the same direction. I'd like to tell you this, Kenyon, that I hope you'll be able to trust me in any pinch—as long as I'm around your part of the world."

Kenyon held out his hand. It was taken in a firm grasp by Silver as they looked fixedly into the eyes of one another.

Then Kenyon began to laugh out of pure pleasure.

"It's been a lucky day for me—a right lucky day—if only poor Jerry hadn't gone! But Jerry was twelve, and every year it was harder for him to do what he wanted and live up to himself. Well, there he was, out fighting on the danger line, and that's the way that he would have chosen to die, I guess. And I'll tell you what, Arizona—the Indians all used to believe that when a brave went up to the happy hunting ground, he was sure to find his best horses there before him, waiting."

He laughed again in some embarrassment, as though he disclaimed a belief in any such superstition. But for a time, as they walked along, his eyes went upward and roved the sky with a blowing rack of clouds, and with such a smile on his lips that Silver knew suddenly what thoughts were running in the mind of his simple friend.

Silver made a fierce and a deep resolve to give mind and heart and hand to this man until that call which moved him irresistibly across the face of the world reached him again, and drew him he knew not where across the sky line.

He was still thinking of this hours later, when they came over a hill into sight of a town, and down a trail not far from them a woman was riding.

"Look!" cried Kenyon. "There's Mustang—and there's Edith Alton! Do you need more'n a sight of the way of her to tell that there's no other woman like her on earth?"

Chapter III

EDITH ALTON

MUSTANG was a flourishing center of trade, as was proved by the five roads that led into it, all whitened by constant travel, to say nothing of the irregular trails that were traced threadlike over the surrounding hills. Mustang Creek darted through the midst of the town, with two bridges over its narrow banks, and scattered groves of pines came down from the hills and right into the town itself. What more could the heart of any mountaineer require than such profusion of wood and water? Moreover, the town was placed where it could serve the great mountain region that tumbled behind it to the north and west, and also send out its freighters through the plains beyond the southern and the eastern hills.

But Silver gave that picture only a glance. Neither did he regard the huge wagon, drawn by fourteen mules, that was rolling down one of the white roads toward Mustang, sending the screech of brakes, like the screaming of hawks or bagpipes, through the still air toward him. What he watched was the girl who came pitching down a trail on the other side of the valley, swerving her horse through brush and among boulders, with the wind of the gallop fanning the brim of her sombrero straight up, and her bandanna fluttering behind her neck like a flag.

"And that's Edith Alton?" said Silver thoughtfully, shaking his head a little. "She's a Western girl, then, Kenyon?"

"No more Western," said Kenyon, grinning, "than Boston and New York. But she's the sort that knows how to do what other folks do, wherever she goes. She could ride Eastern, and it don't take much for them to learn to ride Western. I've stood and seen her, Arizona—I've stood and seen her thrown four times hand running from a pitching broncho, and get up and take the saddle, and never pull leather till that mustang fitted to her like a silk glove and said 'Yes' and 'No' just the way she wanted! And there she goes, sailing. And that black mare of hers is a piece of silk all over, too. I'd know that mare, and I'd know that girl, by the sassy way they've got about them!"

Silver let this talk slip easily through his mind while he studied the disappearing rider. She rode, in fact, as though she had been raised in the saddle. Some of the dark suspicion went out of Silver's heart, for what Western man can resist the sight of a woman who knows how to ride "straight up and hell bent"?

"She looks like one in a million," he said to Kenyon. "I suppose you've wanted to paint her or do her in words!"

"Paint her? Me? I can paint a barn; I wouldn't aim to even paint a house except on a bet. Words? I've written ten letters in my life, I guess, and that's about all!"

It seemed to Silver that the last possible way of understanding Kenyon's hold on this girl had been removed. If there had been mystery before, it was doubly dark now.

They came down into the village, Kenyon explaining why he had been riding across country. He had gone to the nearest railroad to telegraph to his distant parents the news of his approaching wedding, and to buy in a larger town a suit of store clothes that would be a credit to him when he "stood up in church." But when he and Silver had examined the pack behind the saddle of the dead Jerry, they had found it almost totally consumed.

"It don't matter so much," declared Kenyon. "She ain't the kind to care much about clothes. They wouldn't make much difference to her! It's the other things that count with her."

Every word he spoke, every expression of trust and faith, pulled at the heart of Silver as though he heard them spoken by a child who was about to be disillusioned in this savage world of facts.

They went to the hotel.

"The time you get straightened up," said Kenyon, "I'll tell her that you're coming in to eat supper with us in the dining room. She'll be right glad. There's only one other thing. She wants the wedding to be a surprise to everybody back home; everybody that knows her. She don't want it to be talked about here. You'll understand how it is, Arizona?"

Silver nodded and smiled, but his smile was very faint; and as he heard this, something rang like a bell in his mind, and made him surer than ever that the whole thing was a cruel illusion which was being built up around his companion.

After watering the stallion, Silver put Parade into the stable behind the hotel, and saw that he was well-fed with clean hay of barley and wild oats. After that he took a room in the hotel and went up to shave and wash and brush his clothes clean of the dust of the long walk.

He was not tired. That body of his was furnished with steel springs so tempered that no ordinary strain could make an impression on him. And now, with a light step, he went down into the lobby and waited in the little square hall.

The girl came first. He watched her down the stairs. If all the features of her picture had been blurred, he told himself that he would have known her by something high and proud in the carriage of her head. And though she wore a plain khaki riding skirt and the most ordinary of blue silk blouses with full sleeves that ended at the elbows, she seemed dressed for the pleasure of the most critical eye in the world.

She was a smiling girl, of the sort that people like to see even in a stage or a railroad carriage, or in a ballroom, or on a street, merely. Glances trailed after her, and strange expressions of homesickness appeared for a fading moment in the faces of the men in the lobby.

She seemed to know the names of most of them, and she spoke to them all. In another part of the world she would have been surrounded at once, but in the West a woman generally "belongs" to some man, and outsiders are not in haste to rush in and make fools of themselves. She came straight across to Silver and held out her hand.

"Ned told me about you," she said. "You're Arizona, and you don't bother about other names except Jim. And he told me how you saved him from the fire, and that you're going to have supper with us so that I can thank you."

He looked straight back into her eyes. As far as he could penetrate them, there was nothing but candor. And yet there was a trick somewhere. It could not be honest. It must be a sham. She had blue eyes, a little stained with shadow on the lower lids, almost as though with a cosmetic. Her brow was as clear as a sculptor's marble. He could not find a place to put his finger and say that this or that might be the sign and the symbol of deceit. And her beauty drew at him like the first day of spring after a long, white winter.

"I don't want thanks," he said. "I've had a chance to talk to Kenyon, and I've learned to know him a little on the way here. That's better than having thanks."

She sat down beside him, explaining that Kenyon would be with them later. It seemed to Silver that perhaps she had turned to her chair a little too quickly, when she heard this deliberate praise of her fiancé. She went on to say that it generally took Ned a good bit of time to get his hair in order.

"It sticks up like fingers around the crown," she said, and laughed a little.

Silver did not laugh. He was looking back into his brain, running over his memories of other women. There had been none that gave a clew to her. There was an air of perfect calmness, of self-possession and strength, that set her apart from the rest.

She was talking again, in spite of his silence. Her whole attitude was one of gratitude and almost of reverence, though she would not touch again on the thing he had done that day for Kenyon.

Outside, the sunset was drawn red across the window. He wished that the full light of the day were striking about them, and that he could keep studying her face. But perhaps it was better this way, for he could face almost away from her and still regard her from the corner of his eye. That is an art. The cultivation of it had saved the life of Silver on more than one day.

She was saying: "Ned tells me that you don't talk about the past; that it's all future with you, Arizona. But I suppose that you've been what every one is out here, part prospector, cow-puncher, lumberman?"

He turned up the palm of his hand. The fingers were straight and lithe, as the fingers of a child. There were no callouses. Labor never had deformed that supple hand.

"No," he said simply.

And for the first time he had touched her. It was only a single upward flash of her eyes, and perhaps she felt that she was shielded from his observation because he was not directly facing her. But in that flash he thought he read suspicion and sudden fear.

He explained his simple negative. "I'm one of the drifters. I'm one of the idlers. I've daubed a rope on a cow now and then; and I've chipped rock with a hammer, too, and swung an ax now and then. But business never has interfered with pleasure."

"And pleasure?" she asked.

"Pleasure?" said he. "Oh, it comes in its own form. I never can tell where I'll find it, or what it will be like. To-morrow I ought to find it, though, when I see you stand up before the preacher with my friend, Kenyon."

She did not wince. She did not blush. She began to

nod a little, and she kept on smiling. But he felt that the smile was a trifle, a trifle too fixed.

All of his suspicions took him by the throat. What she could possibly gain from a marriage with Kenyon he could not guess. But in that instant he was convinced that it was not the man she wanted, but something else that she would reach through him.

And all her beauty seemed to drop away from her suddenly, as though a hailstorm had swept across the spring day of which she had reminded him, darkening the skies in a moment and battering grass and flowers into a common mud. So it was for Silver in that instant, and he could face her now with his own faint smile, that seemed to come from nothing except sunshiny content of the heart. It would be a contest between them, and in the angry mood that possessed him, he almost pitied the girl who sat there, still smiling, still making pleasant conversation. The ice already must be entering her heart. She had guessed that he was hostile. She must be choosing the weapons with which she would fence.

Far back in his mind he cast, to find some possible goal of the deception she was practicing on poor Ned Kenyon. Silver could think of none unless it were a matter of property. And what property would a man like Kenyon be apt to have? He must make inquiry about that.

Kenyon came down. They went into the dining room together. They sat at the table, and made conversation amiably until poor Kenyon fell into a silence and merely stared hungrily at the girl.

If she were embarrassed, Silver helped her at that moment, for he began to tell stories of old Mexico that soon had both of the others agape with excitement.

Afterward they went out onto the veranda to watch the moonlight that poured down into the valley, making the upper branches of the pines a luminous mist. Kenyon went to buy tobacco for his pipe. And she said to Silver, in the shadow that covered them:

"Why are you against me? Why are you hating me?

Why are you getting ready to crush me in the palm of your hand?"

He merely looked down at her and said nothing. Then he drew on his cigarette to complete, in this way, the perfection of the insult, and so that by the glowing tip of the cigarette she would be able to see his face dimly lighted, and his smile.

Chapter IV

AT THE LONE STAR

AFTER Ned Kenyon returned, the girl remained with them only a short time. When she had excused herself and said good night, Silver was left alone with his new friend. He found Kenyon overflowing with questions. It was not that the man doubted the beauty, the grace, the wonder of the girl, but it was simply that he preferred hearing Silver reassure him, because there was no other subject in the world of half so much importance to him. It was for the moment the subject that was most on the mind of Silver, also; but he wanted silence to think the thing over. He was glad when Kenyon suggested a drink.

They went across the street diagonally into the Lone Star Saloon and found a dozen men leaning their elbows on the bar. Luck favored them in finding a vacant space at the extreme end. Silver put his back against the wall.

It was the ordinary type of saloon, the room long and narrow, with a few tables against the wall, and a strewing of sawdust on the floor.

Silver had barely taken his place when he heard a voice say:

"Is that Kenyon?"

"That's him," said another. "Wanta be introduced?"

"I don't hanker to have nobody introduce me to a skunk," said the first speaker. "I'll introduce myself with the toe of my boot. Because I'm goin' to kick some new wrinkles into his spinal column."

By this time the attention of the entire saloon was focused on the fellow. He was one of the "picturesque"

26

Western types, with blond, saber-shaped mustache, and
a lean face a little too pale to belong to an honest man
in this part of the world, unless he had just risen from
a sick bed. He wore the finest of shopmade boots; his
shirt was of yellow silk; and above all, his revolver had
a handle of shining pearl. Yet it was apparently not a
tenderfoot's gun worn for show, but a useful tool. The
way the holster was buckled about the thigh showed
that, and the low pitch of the gun, angling forward a
trifle so that the butt would be conveniently ready for a
whipsnap draw. If ever this fellow worked, it was fairly
apparent that his business must have to do with Colt
revolvers.

He was coming forward now, and Silver took heed
of Kenyon as the acid test was about to be applied to
him. There are few grimmer moments than that in
which a man is asked to defend his personal dignity
and life from the attack of an armed stranger.

Ned Kenyon turned gray with fear and shuddered,
so that the heart of Silver sickened. He closed his eyes
for an instant, to shut out the picture of that terror.

And *this* was the man that Edith Alton had said she
would marry the next day?

The bartender glanced at Kenyon and then shook
his head.

"What's the matter, Buck?" he asked gently.
"Kenyon never makes no trouble for nobody!"

"Buck" kicked a chair out of his path. It caromed
across the floor and crashed against the wall.

"That's what *you* say, you square-headed fool of a
beer-drinking Dutchman!" cried Buck. "But I say different. And I got in mind right now to ask Mr. Kenyon
to up and say is he a sneaking skunk or ain't he?"

Ned Kenyon turned around slowly. Silver half expected him to bolt for the door. Instead, his voice came
out thin and sharp through the nose, but with a tone
steady enough.

"I don't know you, Buck," said Ned Kenyon. "And
I guess you don't know me. But anyway you look at it,
I'm a peaceable fellow. I don't want trouble."

"I'm askin' you," said Buck, "are you a hound, or ain't you a hound? And if you ain't a hound, how you goin' to prove that to me? Hey?"

He thrust out his head. His lips twitched back to show the yellow line of his teeth. He was cold sober, and he was doing his best to work himself into a fighting rage.

Kenyon sighed very audibly.

"Well," he said, "I take everybody to witness that I'm not hunting for a fight. I never have in my life. I never so much as pointed a gun at any man. But on the other hand, I guess I never took water, that I can recollect, and I don't aim to start taking it now."

Silver, bewildered and delighted, could hardly believe his ears. Buck, also, was so amazed that he halted for an instant. Then a swift flash of joy crossed his face. For after this speech of Kenyon's, the fight that was to be would be in the nature of a fair battle, fairly accepted—the sort of thing which too often passes as "self-defense" west of the Mississippi.

At the same time, the men along the bar who had been looking on curiously, now scattered rapidly back toward the wall, to be out of the line of a possible gun play. The bartender prepared to duck.

It was strange to see how calmly every one took this incident. Mustang, to be sure, was "wide open"; but even if the inhabitants had not seen gun fights before, they had heard of them often enough to brace their nerves for the shock.

Ned Kenyon stood straight and stiff. The straightness pleased Silver. The stiffness told him beforehand that his friend would die.

He took Kenyon by the shoulder and gently, irresistibly, pulled him out of the way. His left elbow was leaning on the bar. He continued to lean there, at ease with his right hand resting on his hip.

"Buck," said Silver, "if you want to talk, talk to me, will you?"

"There ain't anybody that I won't talk to," said Buck. "Who in the devil are you?"

"I'll tell you a part of what I am," said Silver. "In a way, I'm your sort of an hombre, Buck. I spend a lot of time every day practicing with my guns, just as you do. I'm an expert. I'm such an expert that I know the average fellow, who does honest work with his hands, can't possibly stand up to me. Ned Kenyon, for one instance, probably couldn't stand up to me, any more than he can stand up to you."

It was perhaps the oddest speech that was ever heard in a Western barroom. It struck every whisper out of the air. Winter frost could not have stilled all life more completely. Only the mouth of the bartender gaped and closed again, like a fish on dry land, making its last gasp for air.

"You're goin' to put yourself in his boots, are you?" said Buck. "You're goin' to prove that he ain't a skunk? You'll have some proving to show me what *you* are!"

"Wait a minute, Arizona," said Ned Kenyon. "This here is mighty fine of you, but I aim to fight my own fights when they come my way."

"Take your hand away from my shoulder!" snapped Silver, sharply, so that Kenyon jumped back. "And don't speak to me again. This rat here is likely to try his teeth on me the first instant he thinks that I'm off guard. Do you hear me, Buck?"

"Hear you? Well, yes!" shouted Buck. He smote the floor with the flat of his foot and swayed forward a little. Then curse began to spill out of his mouth.

"Were you hired to do this?" asked Silver.

The cursing stopped.

"Because," said Silver, "every time you swear, it's going to be harder on you. I thought at first that I might have to pull a gun and put you to sleep, Buck. But I can see now that I won't have to go that far, because you're only cursing to keep yourself warm, and you wish, this minute, that you were out there in the street in the kind darkness."

Buck tried to laugh. "Just a big bluff and a blowhard," he cried. "And when I break him in two, you'll all see yaller!"

But no one nodded. No one smiled in sympathy with Buck's laugh. It had been too hollow and manifestly false.

"I'm going to ask you a few questions," said Silver. "If you don't answer them, I'll give you a quirting. But in the first place, I'll have to take your gun away from you. Put up your hands, Buck."

He said this so quietly, with such assurance, that the spectators gaped and craned their necks, and could hardly believe that Silver did not have his man covered.

"Why, you fool!" shouted Buck. "You think I'm crazy?"

"You don't think that," said Silver. "You know I'm right, and that I'll do what I say. You know that I'm a faster hand and a surer shot than you are, Buck. And your poor little soul is shrinking and dying in you. There's a sort of pity that grows up in me when I see you turn white around the mouth, as you're doing now. And a disgust when I see your eyes begin to roll."

He stood straight, and commanded in a harsher voice.

"Put up your hands!"

It was a frightful thing to see that armed man, that gun fighter, that slayer of men—Buck—standing wavering as though a whole regiment of soldiers had drawn a bead on him. But all that threatened him was the empty hand and the pointing finger of Silver.

"You hear me?" said Silver, and took a half step forward.

A queer, bubbling sound broke out of the throat of Buck. His mouth yawned. His lips started to frame words, and could make only a hideous gibberish.

And there before the eyes of the crowd the miracle happened, and his hands started to rise from the level of his pearl-handled revolver to his hips—would he try to whip out some hidden weapon, then?—and so on to his breast, and up to his shoulders, where they fluttered for an instant in feeble revolt, but then continued until they were above the top of his head.

The sickening thing was not finished. Silver stepped forward and pulled the pearl-handled gun out of its sheath, and as he drew it, a great groan of despair came from Buck. He had allowed an act of shame to be performed on him that would make him a very legendary figure of shame, a horror of which no man would gladly speak.

Yet all of those men who watched with pale, fascinated eyes, stared less at Buck in his disgrace than at the terrible face of Silvertip as he pulled that gun out, and then laid it on the bar. And more than one man wondered, if the face of Silver were before him, if he would have had the nerve to do anything other than Buck had done.

Hypnotism was what it seemed like. No man exchanged glances with his neighbor. Each man hoped that his own horror was not being observed, and each knew that the coldness of his skin meant a definite pallor.

"You can get the gun afterward," said Silver. "I'm not going to take it and keep it. And I'm not going to harm you in any way, Buck, so long as you tell me, frankly, the name of the man who hired you for this job. You *were* hired, I take it?"

The jaw of Buck dropped. He gasped, "Yes! Hired! Oh—yes, I was—"

One long breath was drawn by all the men in that room. The bartender stood straight for the first time since Silver had begun speaking.

"Who hired you?" demanded Silver.

"Who? A gent by the name of Alec Wilson."

"You lie!" said Silver. "Kenyon, get me your quirt, will you?"

"Not Wilson!" groaned Buck. "What I meant was, the gent that hired me was really—"

There was an open window at the side of the room. A gun glinted beyond the sill, now, and the explosion of the shot tossed the mouth of the revolver a little up into the air.

The head of Buck dropped over on his shoulder. He slumped into the arms of Silver, slipped out of them, and spilled onto the floor.

Chapter V

THE MURDERER'S NAME

SILVER went out of that room like a cat after a bird, but as he turned the front corner of the building he heard the rapid beating of hoofs begin behind the saloon, and knew that the quarry was on the wing.

Oh, for five minutes of Parade, then—to loose the golden stallion like an arrow at the mark—or for any horse, for that matter. But there were none except down the street, at the hitch rack on the farther side of the hotel, and that was too far away.

He went gloomily back into the saloon. Half the men had scattered to look for the murderer; half had remained to look at the victim.

He was dying, beyond doubt. The bullet had cut straight through his lungs, and Buck was already in his death agony. He kept rising on one hand, and turning his swollen face and his terrible, starting eyes from one man to another, mutely asking help.

But there was no help to be given. The finest doctor in the world could not assist, though messengers had gone to fetch all the physicians in Mustang. Buck himself seemed to realize that there were only seconds to him. Then he tried to speak, and that was the worst of all.

Silver, the indirect cause of his death, was the man he wanted most to talk to. He came clawing across the floor and reached up and caught Silver's hand in his. He tried to speak, but only a rapid succession of red bubbles burst on his lips. He was strangling. He was biting at the air, and getting none down to his lungs.

Others drew back from that sight of agony, but Silver slipped to the floor and sat by the struggling body.

"Write it, Buck!" he called loudly. "Write it on the floor! Write the name, and I swear that I'll try to get him for you!"

Buck was beating on the floor with his feet and hands, in the last struggle between death and life, but he understood Silver. He flopped heavily over on his side, dipped his right forefinger into the thick pool of his own blood, and commenced to write. Then death caught back his redstained hand and turned him on his back. He seemed to be making a last effort to speak as he died. One long shudder ran through his body, and he was gone.

On the floor beside him was written: "Nel—" followed by the sweeping stroke of crimson where his finger had been snatched from the writing.

Silver folded the hands of the dead man across his breast and closed the half-open eyes. When he looked up, he saw that men were standing by with their hats in their hands, and with sick faces.

He stood up and took off his own hat.

"Does anybody here know a woman named Nell, or a man named Nelson?" he asked.

"There's a woman that does laundry," said the bartender, instantly.

Silver shook his head.

"There's Digger Nelson, the prospector," said another in the room.

"What sort of a man?" asked Silver.

"A regular rock chipper. He patches the seat of his pants with flour sacks and—"

"No!" said Silver. "He's not the man I want. He's not the man who hired Buck to pick a fight with Ned Kenyon, and shoot it out. He's not that sort."

The first of the doctors came hurrying in. The sheriff was just at his heels. Silver took Ned Kenyon by the arm and led him out of the barroom into a back room, closing the door behind them. They sat down at a table.

Mustang was now well awakened. Scores of footfalls were padding up the street, or pounding loudly over the board sidewalks. Horses snorted in the distance under the spur. Voices were gathering toward the saloon like buzzing bees toward the hive. Presently the sheriff would be sure to want both Silver and Kenyon, but Silver used this interim to pump Kenyon as well as he could.

"Ned," he said, "do you know what to make of all this?"

"I'm flabbergasted," said poor Kenyon. "I can't make head or tail of it. But it looks as though you know the inside workings of everything!"

"I wish I did! I'm only guessing. I'm reaching into the dark and getting at nothing. That's all! Nothing! Ned, listen to me!"

"The way I would to a preacher," said Kenyon, with a naïveté that made Silver faintly smile.

"What does this fellow Buck hitch with?"

"I don't make that out, either. I never saw him before. I don't suppose that he ever saw me. He says that he was hired—"

Into this stream of meaningless words Silver broke sharply.

"What's the thing we can catch on?" he asked. "There's something you have, or that you're about to have, that other people want—or want to keep you from. Now tell me out and out—have you anything worth money?"

"Not even a horse," said the stage driver sadly. "Not even Jerry, now!"

"You have some land, somewhere," suggested Silver.

"Father has a patch—a quarter section. That's all there is in the family."

"Where? In the mountains? Some place where pay dirt might be found? Gravel, for instance? Near an old creek bed, perhaps?"

"Pay dirt? The clay runs down about a thousand feet. The old man works that ground about sixteen hours a day, and he hardly makes a dollar a day, clear.

I never saw worse clay. We've dug wells. We know how far that clay goes down."

"Wait a moment," said Silver, violently readjusting the course of his suspicions. "There's another chance. You've been around the world a good deal, partner. And you're sure to know a good lot. You've looked in on some queer things in your time. You've seen men in odd positions. You have up your sleeve something that some one would be pretty glad to hush up. Think, now. It must be that!"

Kenyon thought. After his fashion, he took his time, fixing his eyes on distance, and thoroughly combing his memory. At last he said: "No. There's nothing that I can put a finger on."

"There must be," insisted Silver. "There has to be something! Think again."

"No, Arizona—or Jim, if I can call you that—there's nothing. Nothing ever happens to me—or nothing ever did happen until—"

"All right," said Silver. "That brings us back to Edith Alton, as far as I can see. You're going to marry her to-morrow morning. And some one hates the idea of that. Somebody wants to stop you. Somebody with a first or a last name beginning with Nel. Who could it be?"

Again Kenyon shook his head. "I don't know. It beats me."

"It beats you? It'll *kill* you before you're many days older!" said Silver. "Man, man, are you sure that you don't know anyone whose name begins with those three letters?"

"Well, Jim," said Kenyon, "don't be mad at me. I'm trying to think, but there are not many people whose name begins with those letters."

"No," said Silver. "There are not many. That's good point in the deal. It'll narrow down the hunting field."

"You *look* like a hunter," said Kenyon, rather overawed. "But by the jumping thunder, Jim, I'd hate to have you on my trail with that look in your eye and with that set to your jaw!"

"I'm not on your trail. I'm on the trail of murder," said Silver. "I can smell the murder inside my nostrils. I can taste it against the roof of my mouth. Murder— *phaugh!*"

The door opened. There stood on the threshold a man with a stocky body and a long, triangular face.

"Murder is what we been talking about, in there," he said. "Maybe I can talk to you two boys in here about the same thing."

Others were about to follow this stranger inside the room, but he closed the door in their faces, and they did not try to open it behind his back.

He came across the floor, opening his coat to show the badge that was pinned inside it.

"Name of Philips," he said. "Or maybe you'll introduce me, Ned?"

Kenyon started up and sawed the air with his hand, embarrassed.

"This here is Sheriff Philips. Bert Philips," he said. "And this is a friend of mine that's got into a lot of trouble on my account, this day. He's Arizona Jim, sheriff. And he—"

He paused. The inadequacy of that nickname seemed to fill the throat of Kenyon, at the moment that he spoke to the man of the law.

"Glad to know you, Arizona," said the sheriff. "Ned, who killed Buck?"

"I don't know. I wish—"

"Ever have a grudge between you?"

"Never. I never saw him before he—"

"Ned, you walk out and buy yourself a drink. I want to talk with Arizona."

Ned Kenyon went out hesitantly, as one who feels that he may be deserting a friend in a time of need, but the calm smile of Silver reassured him until the door was opened and closed again.

Then the sheriff pulled out a chair and sat down opposite Silver. He said: "You know what I've got on my knee?"

"Yes," said Silver. "A gun."

"Does that mean anything to you?"

"It means that you're rather young," said Silver.

The sheriff frowned. Then, suddenly, he grinned.

"You're all they say about you,—Silver," he said.

Silver said nothing at his identification by the man of the law.

"A dead cool one," continued the sheriff. "Now, you tell me who killed Buck."

Silver smiled.

"Go on!" urged the sheriff.

"Otherwise you'll shoot?"

Suddenly Philips raised the gun into view and shoved it back inside his coat.

"Maybe I've been a fool," he said. "I thought for a minute that I'd call your bluff. But now I almost think you mean what you've been saying. That right?"

"It is."

"You're Kenyon's friend?"

"Yes."

"Do you make anything out of this mess, then?"

"Only guesses."

"Let's have them, Silver. I don't know just how to take you. There's some call you a crook and a man-killer, and others say that you're the whitest man on earth. Anyway, you have brains, and you've been a friend to poor Ned Kenyon. Now, tell me everything you think."

"I think," said Silver, "that some one wants to stop a thing that's due to happen to Kenyon to-morrow."

"What?"

"I can't tell you. I've promised Kenyon not to tell."

"Stop him by killing him?"

"Gladly, if there's no other way."

"Silver, how much do you know?"

"Hardly more than a baby."

The sheriff laid hold of his chin with a big brown hand and gripped hard, staring over his knuckles at the face of Silver.

"It's hard," he said, "but I'm going to believe you. I want to know this: Are you working with me?"

"With all my might!"

"Good!" said the sheriff. "And if you have an idea, you can call on me night or day."

"I'll have an idea before the end of to-morrow," said Silver. "And then I may call on you to blow up half this town!"

Chapter VI

DAWN RIDING

SILVER went to his room, dipped a towel in cold water, tied it around his head, and waited for the whisky fumes to disappear. He had had only two drinks, but he felt that they were too many. He sat in the darkness, without a lamp, watching the moonlight inch its way across the floor, reach the feet of a chair, and crawl up the varnished legs.

But still he could find no answer to the questions which were whirling in his mind.

He took off his boots, left his room, and went down the stairs. The outer doors were all locked. He opened a window, got onto the veranda, and stole down it until he stepped onto the pine needles beneath the grove beside the building. There he sat with his back to a tree, not even smoking, and watched the moonlight shine on the windows of the house as on pools of black water.

The moon grew dim. Its shadows no longer made a pattern of jet and white on the ground. The dawn came, with a chill that started his flesh quaking, and then he heard the loud rattling of iron on iron, as some one began to work at the kitchen stove. Immediately afterward, a door in the back of the hotel groaned faintly.

Silver got up, and walked behind the trees until he could see the small form of a woman hurrying toward the barn. He knew her by the walk—the girl who was to marry Ned Kenyon before noon of this day.

He rounded to the back of the stable. Two seconds after she led out the black mare he was on Parade. He was saddling as she turned down the main street of Mustang, and he was able to note the direction. A half minute later he was riding west, also, but keeping behind the most outlying houses of the town. In that way, he rounded into the head of the valley in time to see the rose of the morning bloom on all the snow-clad peaks of the distance. A solitaire was singing as though the beauty of the dawn had filled its heart. And in the distance he saw the black horse slide into the shadows of a big grove of pines.

He followed only a short distance up the valley, for he was reasonably sure, for a definite reason, that she would ride up the same trail by which he had seen her descend the evening before. Kenyon had told him that she loved to ride out by herself—generally toward the west. That was her favorite, the zigzag trail down the western hills, Kenyon had remarked.

But it would be very odd if she preferred that trail to others that were ten times more beautiful. And if she was, as Kenyon said, merely a girl tenderfoot trying to see the west for herself unimpeded by too much chaperonage, it would have been more natural for her to take all of the trails, one by one. Some singular attraction had kept her until deep into the evening of the day before among those western hills. Perhaps the same thing—not the beauty of the morning—was taking her out there before the day had well begun.

Silver rode up the slope to the left of him to the water divide above. The black mare was fast, but she could not keep pace with the cat feet and the winged stride of the golden stallion. Parade was well over the ridge and coming through a group of trees, when Silver saw the girl swinging her horse at an angle across his line. And he sighed with content. He was on the right trail. And if she were ten thousand times more beautiful than she was, he would find her share in the mystery and lay it bare.

So he shadowed her, moving Parade with care from one covert to another, half guessing the probable course of the girl a dozen times, and always hitting it correctly.

She dipped into a narrow ravine, at last, and Silver had to halt his horse on the brink of the steep ground, then rein it well back to wait for the black mare to climb out up the farther bank.

He waited a sufficient time, until a pinch of suspicion stirred him. So he dismounted, put Parade in a clump of tall brush, gave him the word that would tether him in place more strongly than ropes, and went forward on foot to investigate.

He had to lie flat and peer over the rim of the canyon, before he could see what he wanted. But the sight was reward, and a rich one. For in a clearing among the trees in the middle of the ravine he saw the girl walking up and down with a young man in a gray felt hat with a brim foolishly narrow for Western weather, and with a quick step, and nervous gestures. That was all that Silver could make out.

The stranger seemed to be pouring out a tirade, to which the girl listened most of the time with a bent head. She seemed then to be making gestures of denial, and at this he fell into an attitude of earnest argument and persuasion, until the very ears of Silver ached to hear the words.

Whatever they were, they were sufficient. Presently she was nodding in agreement, and then she was putting her head up in its characteristic fearless poise, as though she were ready to outface the world.

A few minutes later, the two disappeared under the trees, and then the black mare mounted the farther slope and tipped out over the rim of it beyond his view.

There remained the fellow in the ravine. Silver worked down the sharp slope toward him, moving more like a snake than a man. It was hard to make that descent with any surety that he was unseen, for a dozen times he was without real cover. He was perhaps twenty steps from the bottom of the valley when a rifle clanged, a bullet spatted against the ground beside his face, and he had to dive into the shrubbery before him as into water.

He was worming his way through that cover, with his revolver in his hand, when he heard the rapid thudding of hoofs that ranged up the ravine, and knew his quarry had taken to flight.

Gloomily he went on until he came to a small clearing in which a mere dog tent was pitched. There was a heap of empty cans, at one side. There was a rudely put together fireplace built of stones. And under the cover of the tent he saw a bed made down, the blankets rumpled, together with a book or two and a few magazines.

Silver went around the camp with a furtive step. This camper had been on the spot for a week, at least. He was not used to a life in the open, or he would have built his fireplace better. He was no fisherman, for he would have worn a trail along the side of the little brook, and particularly down to the edge of the broad, still pool not far away. He was, in fact, nothing but a tenderfoot.

Silver sat down on a stump and smoked a cigarette. He had plenty of facts, and he could make a few deductions.

The girl who was betrothed to Kenyon came to this place daily, so it seemed, in order to talk with a light-stepping, active young man who apparently was able to persuade her against her will on matters of importance. This young gentleman, instead of going to the hotel in the town, preferred to live in the wilderness, though he had neither talent nor apparent liking for that life—for no one who liked it could have put up with the arrangements of that camp. In addition to these things, there was the further fact that the stranger actually had tried with his rifle for the life of a man who was stealing upon his camp!

The component parts made the picture of one who could not be other than a criminal, it seemed to Silver. And if he were, it was a fact that threw keen light upon the character of the girl.

But with this much gained, Silver had to return to Mustang. He went back to Parade, and took a leisurely way to the town, his mind crammed with thought every inch of the way. In the stable behind the hotel, he put up the stallion and paused to look over the mare. She had been taken flying home. She still was head down, panting hard, and the sweat was still running on her sleek body. It was apparent that the girl had wished to be away from the hotel as short a time as possible.

Silver went up to his room, undressed, slipped into his bed, turned on his face, and slept soundly for two hours. Then the striking of the breakfast gong roused him.

A wash in cold water wakened him thoroughly. He dressed, and went down the stairs humming softly, and into the dining room, where the girl and Ned Kenyon were already having bacon and eggs, with a sooty pot of coffee beside them, for service in that hotel was not of the most polite.

"A good night, Arizona?" asked the girl cheerfully.

"One of the best," said Silver. "Did you sleep right through?"

"Like the dead!" said she, and smiled at him.

It was a good, direct smile, with open eyes that met his, easily. He wanted to say to her: "You lie well. I know the types of liars, and you're one of the best!"

Yet, as he sat there with them, as he heard the softness of her voice, as he watched the clear beauty of her face, he found himself saying, against his better judgment, that she must be all right. It would be an irony, a sarcasm of nature, if she were other than honest and true.

Poor Ned Kenyon, who dwelt on her with his eyes, who devoured her every gesture, every word from her throat—what would he say if he knew of that visitation to the stranger over the hills?

Silver had a chance to find out, a few moments later, when the girl finished and excused herself from the table. As she rose from her place, her glance lingered for one serious, penetrating instant on the face of Silver. Then she went out hastily, as though not trusting the words that she was tempted to speak.

Afterward, Silver said, to the rapt face of Ned Kenyon: "You love her, son."

"More'n breath," said Kenyon simply.

"If she turned out to be a counterfeit—would that stop you?"

Kenyon did not smile. He merely looked out the window for a moment, as though to contemplate the immensity of that suggestion in a calm seriousness.

Then he said: "You're a swimmer, Jim?"

"Yes," said Silver.

"You know what it means," said Kenyon, "to fetch under water for a long distance?"

Silver nodded.

"And the way your lungs burn—and all? Well, suppose that you came up to the surface and there was no air to breathe! And it's that way with me. It ain't what is right or wrong about her, any more. It's just that I couldn't live without her in every day of my life—either having her, being with her, or knowing all the time that she belongs to me. You see?"

"I see," said Silver.

"Murder," said Kenyon quietly, "not even if she'd done murder, it wouldn't stop me. It'd matter, but it'd matter as though I'd done it myself. That's all. But what was in your mind, partner?"

"Well, I was just thinking, was all," said Silver. "I simply wanted to know how you felt."

"In a couple of hours," murmured Kenyon, "there's a new life waiting for me. I'm not thinking about that. I don't dare. It's like thinking of walking on water, or walking on blue air. But you'll be there, Jim. You'll be there to steady me. That's what I'm counting on."

Silver got out of the room like a blind man, fumbling. For he knew that to tell his friend of what he had seen this morning would be like pouring acid on a man already incurably ill. He could not speak!

Chapter VII

THE WEDDING

THE church was a little square frame box with a steeple tacked onto one side of it, like a forefinger lifted above a fist. The preacher was a good, hard-working man who covered all parts of his parish both winter and summer, climbing among ice-clad rocks in winter to places that no horse or mule could ever reach. Only a small percentage of Mustang attended his Sunday services, but there was not a man in the district who would not have fought for the sky pilot.

Silver looked on him with wonder. He was regarding all things with astonishment, at that moment, for he could not believe that Kenyon and the girl were actually standing in front of the man of God, about to be joined in wedlock. The hotel proprietor was one witness. The keeper of the general merchandise store was the other. As for Silver, he had dodged the duty. In case he served, his real name would have to be written down, and that name he preferred to keep unknown.

He stood in the back of the empty little church, acutely aware of the four windows that looked in on the scene, and prepared any instant to see the gleam of a gun outside the glass, for if they had killed one man in the cause of preventing the marriage, did it not stand to reason that they would kill another?

So, with a sense of the two revolvers that hung beneath his armpits, Silver waited, and watched, and was all eyes rather than ears. Yet he could hear the responses, too, and he could be aware of the surprised face which the minister kept continually turning toward

Kenyon. Even that unworldly man could see the absurdity of such a match.

All had been done quietly. Not a soul in the village knew of what was to take place. That was the reason why the church was not crowded.

He heard the preacher saying: "You promise to love, honor and obey—"

Silver saw the girl turn her head suddenly, and flash her eyes at Kenyon before she answered in a forced, barely audible voice: "I do."

Poor Kenyon!

It was over, suddenly. In turn, the witnesses bent to sign the little book. The preacher was shaking hands with the bride and groom. And out of a few spoken words there had been established a bond which should last until death. But would it last for even a day?

Silver watched them come down the aisle. Kenyon was a man walking above the surface of this earth. The girl was pale, with a frozen smile. A careless eye might have put her pallor down to mere timidity, but Silver saw, or felt he saw, that it was an agony of the mind that moved her.

Silver himself avoided shaking hands with them, first by opening the door for them, then by saying that he would hurry to the hotel, and see that the buckboard was ready. For the plan of Kenyon was to take her at once out of Mustang, and then over the green plains and up to the little town where his mother and father lived. It would be a simple honeymoon, but it was all that his purse could afford.

At the hotel, Silver harnessed the span of mustangs which Kenyon had bought to the small buckboard. He heaped in the baggage behind the seat, while Kenyon came out of the hotel to help where he could. But his hands were helpless, and his small eyes were continually lifting to the sky, and being dazzled until they filled with moisture.

The girl would be down in a moment from her room, Kenyon said.

But she did not come for five minutes, for ten minutes, for half an hour.

"Women have always got fixings to go through," said Kenyon. "It don't matter. I'd rather wait for her here than dance with anybody else while a band was playin'."

Silver said abruptly: "Perhaps I can help her about something."

"No. Leave her be. Let her take her time," said Kenyon.

But Silver was already through the door of the hotel. Once out of sight, he moved fast, up the stairs, and to the door of the girl's room. He knocked. There was no answer. He pushed the door open, and no sign of Edith Alton was inside. Only a wraith of white smoke hung in the air above the little round-bellied stove that stood in a corner. And on the table was an envelope, sealed, and addressed in her handwriting to Edward Kenyon.

Silver went down to the back of the hotel and found the cook.

"See Miss Alton go out toward the barn?" he asked.

"Half an hour ago she rode her black mare out of the barn and went up the valley," said the cook. "She was traveling fast, too, like she wanted to catch a train."

Silver came through the hotel to Kenyon and took him by the arm.

"Ned," he said crisply. "you've got bad news. She's left you."

Kenyon straightened. It reminded Silver of how the man had stood the night before, in the saloon—straight, ready to meet his fate, but unable to struggle against it.

"She's left a letter for you upstairs," said Silver. "That may do a little explaining. I'll wait for you down here."

The stone-gray lips of Kenyon parted stiffly. He put a hand on the shoulder of his friend.

"If you wouldn't mind, Jim," said he, "if it wouldn't

be wrong for me to ask, I'd like to have you come up there with me."

That was why Silver climbed the stairs again, suddenly feeling old and weak.

Yet there would be a sufficient strength in him, he thought, if he could lay eyes on the girl, or on that fellow in the hills, who moved with that alert and springing step.

It seemed to Silver now that he had done everything wrong. He should have spoken his suspicions to Kenyon at once. At least he should have demanded from the girl an explanation of her morning visit to that rifleman in the hills—that young fellow who was so ready to try his hand at murder!

But now there was a ruin, and it was entirely in the life and the heart of poor Ned Kenyon.

When they got into the room, Kenyon paused a moment at the door, and took off his hat, breathing deeply.

"Kind of fragrant, Jim, ain't it?" said he. "I mean the air. Kind of like her. Like flowers, eh?"

He actually smiled at Silver, to invite his agreement. But Silver, jerking his hat a little lower on his head, stalked to the window and looked down to the ruts in the dusty street, and across the roofs of the houses, above which the heat waves were shimmering and dancing. He could have drunk hot blood.

He looked sidewise, curiously, at the stove, above which the wraith of smoke was dissolving. In winter weather in Mustang there would be plenty of need for stoves, but hardly at this time of the year. He opened the door. On the fire grate there was a ball of gray-and white fluff, the ashes of small bits of paper which had been wadded together. Now the draft took hold of them and blew them dissolving up the chimney.

He opened the lower door to the ash pan and pulled the pan out. As he had expected, several of the small bits of the paper had dropped through. He picked them up. It was contemptible to read them, but the girl was no longer fit to be treated as a decent human being.

She was a criminal, and she had committed her crime in the most detestable fashion, against the most helpless of men.

So he stared at the few words which he found. Several of the scraps were covered with words written in the more smoothly flowing and smaller hand of a man. None were in her own writing. But of them all there was only one out of which he could make any sense. It contained the words:

out fail in Kirby Cr

That could be pieced out a little. "Without fail in Kirby Creek," was perhaps the true sense of it. Suppose one went back a little and filled in: "Meet without fail in Kirby Creek."

If that referred to the past, it was nothing. If it referred to the future, it might be everything.

"Maybe you better read it," said Kenyon. He was holding out a letter toward Silver. Then he drew back his hand, murmuring: "I dunno, Silver. Seems to me maybe it wouldn't be fair to her, hardly, if I was to show her letter to another man?"

"Fair to—*her?*" asked Silver hoarsely.

"Ah, but don't be too hard on her," said Kenyon. "She ain't very old, Jim. And she ain't very used to the world, and you'll see that the world's been hard on her, poor girl!"

"Well," said Silver, in a voice of iron, "do you want me to read the letter, or not?"

"Not if you talk like that," said Kenyon, drawing back his hand.

Silver laughed, in a sort of despair.

"Give me the letter," he said. "I need to read it. I *have* to read it."

"Well," said Kenyon, "I don't think that she'd mind. Only this morning she said to me that I must always stick to you, because there was no other friend that I'd find like you, in the whole world."

"Did she say that?" asked Silver sharply.

"She did, and she had her heart in her voice, and a kind of a pity and a kindness for me in her eyes, Jim. So I guess she wouldn't mind you seeing what she wrote to me. Here it is."

Silver, taking the letter, for a moment could not look at it. His mental preoccupation was too great, as he pondered over what the girl had said. For she could not have been in doubt that he was her enemy, heartily and forever.

He went back to the window and saw, first of all, pinned to the top sheet of the letter, a check made out to Edward Kenyon for ten thousand dollars and signed Edith Alton Kenyon.

Ten thousand dollars!

Some of his walls of reservations were knocked flat as he saw the sum. If she had done Kenyon harm, she had intended to do him good, also.

The letter ran:

Dear Ned: Tomorrow I expect that we shall be married, unless your friend Arizona Jim finds a way to prevent the ceremony; because he loves you, Ned, and he guessed from the first moment when he saw me that I was not honest.

And I'm not. If you're reading this letter, it is because I have married you, and left you, and this is the farewell message.

I suppose that it's human nature to wish to defend ourselves. That's why I'm going to say that I don't think another woman in the world could have stood out against the terrible necessity that was pressing on me. It was a question of life or death. Not my life or death, but that of another person, infinitely of more importance to the world than I am.

I can't even explain farther than this. I only knew that I had to be married, at once. I knew that I had to be married to a kind and honest man who might never forgive me for having wronged him, but who would not pursue me.

That was why I knew I had found some one who

could be of help to me when I found you. I thought of even telling you what I wanted and of asking you to marry me, and then forget me, and divorce me. But I couldn't risk that. You might say no, and then there would be no time to find another man. I had to talk with you, persuade you into asking me to marry you, and then go through with the ceremony.

Then it seemed to me that you were really growing fond of me. And my heart ached to think of it. But I've rushed through with everything, hoping that God would understand that I meant what is right, even if kind, honest, gentle Ned Kenyon would not be able to understand, ever.

I'm leaving a check with you. It isn't hush money. It's simply that I want with all my heart to help you to the thing you wish to have—a small ranch and a chance to lead your own chosen life. I would make it five times or ten times as much, but I know that you would never take the money.

Forgive me, forgive me.

EDITH.

Chapter VIII

ON THE TRAIL

SILVER, as he finished the second reading of that letter, ground his teeth together in a helpless rage. There was a certain ring of honesty to the words. But he would believe nothing. Her troubles were unknown, distant. The grief of Ned Kenyon was a present and immediate thing. Behind her there was certainly a power of wealth. Ten thousand dollars—which she could have made fifty thousand, she said, if she had dreamed that Ned Kenyon would accept it! It argued piled treasures somewhere in her background.

He gave back the letter to Kenyon.

"What do you think, Jim?" asked Kenyon.

"I think," said Silver, "that you're the straightest fellow I ever met. I think, Ned, that I could cut her heart out, and enjoy the job. As for the letter—man, it's easy to write words! Dead easy, I tell you!"

"You won't believe that she's honest?" asked Kenyon.

"Never in the world," said Silver. "She knew that you loved her. A woman can never go wrong about that. And still she went ahead."

"There was a matter of life or death," argued Kenyon.

"Bah!" said Silver. "You'd believe that a frog croaks in a marsh!"

Kenyon shook his head, picked up the letter, detached the check, and put the letter itself into his pocket. The check he tore into small pieces, and threw into the stove.

"She knew that you'd do that, too," said Silver bitterly. "She knew that you'd never take the dirty money. Ah, Ned, you're going with me to find her, if we have to travel around the world. You understand? I'm staying with you until we find her, if it takes the rest of my life!"

"Follow her?" said Kenyon, with a look of mild surprise. "No, no, Jim. I can't follow her. She doesn't want me, and I can't bother her. I can't go after her."

"Are you going to sit down and take your licking— from a pretty little female crook?" demanded Silver.

Kenyon turned slowly toward him.

"You're bigger, stronger, and faster than I am, Jim. But if I ever hear you say a word against her again, I'm going to try to knock your head off! I'm sorry to say that, but it's what I mean."

Silver groaned. "What are you going to do, then?" he asked.

"I don't know," said Kenyon. "Back to driving the stage, I guess, and take up where I left off. The boys will guy me a little, when this marriage is known. But I come from the part of the world where they grow good hickory, Jim!"

He smiled, as he said this, and tears suddenly stung the eyes of Silver.

He took the hand of Kenyon and gripped it hard.

"You're a better sort than I am," said Silver. "I'm getting out of Mustang. One of these days I'll see you again. I'm going on a trip and—so long, old-timer!"

He walked out of the room quickly. When he reached the head of the stairs, he could hear the voice of Kenyon calling after him, but he ran down rapidly. His trail was outward. There were many things to fill his mind, from that man who had hired Buck, whose name began with "Nel," to that light-stepping friend of the girl, and there was the girl herself, and that matter of life and death about which she was so wrought up.

He paid his bill, went out to the stable, and saddled Parade. He was outside the barn before he heard the voice of Kenyon raised high in the distance, calling:

"Arizona! Oh, Arizona!" But he put Parade into a hard gallop.

He cut back into the main street of the village, after a short distance, and stopped in front of the blacksmith shop to make his inquiry, for blacksmiths, next to bartenders, know more news than any one else in the West.

The blacksmith came out, busily tying a bandage about a bleeding finger.

"Where's Kirby Creek?" asked Silver.

"Kerby Creek?" said the blacksmith. "Never heard of it."

"There's a place of that name," said Silver.

"Kirby Creek? Never heard of it."

"Anything else that sounds like Kirby Cr—"

The blacksmith grunted with the profundity of his mental effort. Then he said: "There's Kirby Crossing, if that's what you want to know."

"I *do* want to know," said Silver. "Where is it?"

"Fifty mile back into the hills. Yeah, right back into the mountains. You take the northwest road. You foller along it for twenty mile, and then you come to a trail that branches off to the left and—"

Silver listened to the directions, carefully. He repeated them after his informer and was pronounced letter-perfect. After that, he would never forget. The words would stick like glue in his memory.

So he took the northwest road, keeping Parade along the edge of it where there was no dust and the footing was therefore firmer. Gradually the hills rolled up about him in greater and greater dimensions. He was climbing into the mountains when a rider with a pack mule tethered to the pommel of his saddle came down a cross trail toward the main way on which Silver was traveling.

He was a very big man, with a shag of beard covering his face almost to the eyes. And one of those eyes was covered with a great black leather patch. The size of that horseman made the mustang he rode look hardly bigger than a goat.

Silver, seeing that he was noticed, drew rein, and waited. He had reason to wait, he felt, unless he wanted a bullet through his back, for he had recognized "One-eyed Harry" Bench, from whom, not so very long before, he had taken two good riding horses by dint of not so much of the cash he paid down for them as of a bullet through the soft of One-eyed Harry's shoulder.

So Silver waited at the crossing, in doubt.

Those doubts were scattered in a moment, as big Harry Bench let out a whoop and spurred his mustang to a canter, the mule dangling back grimly on the end of the lead rope. Pulling his tough pony to a halt, One-eyed Harry reached far forward and caught the good right hand of Silver in a grip that threatened to break bones.

"Silver!" he shouted. "Curse me black and white if I ever thought I'd lay an eye on you ag'in. How come, you old rattler, that you're in this part of the range? I thought you was away far north, or away far south. What brings you around here?"

"Just drifting, Harry; just drifting. How are things with you?"

"Better'n ever before," said Harry Bench. "The grouch I had at the world was all let out with the blood that run when you slid that chunk of lead through me, Silver. I done some hating of you, for a spell. But when the news got around to me, and I found out that it was Jim Silver himself that had nicked me—why, there ain't no shame in being put down by Silver himself, is there? Not to my way of thinkin'. The day has been, since then, that gents have seen me stripped and wanted to know where I got the scar on the shoulder, and when they hear that it was a bullet out of Silver's gun, I get a considerable pile of attention, Jim. And the boys, they most generally tell me that I'm lucky not to be wearin' that scar right through the heart, and make no mistake about it. Where are you bound?"

He poured out the words in a hearty torrent, and in

a thundering voice that plainly had been rarely confined to the echoing walls of a room.

"I'm bound for Kirby Crossing," said Silver.

"Kriby Crossing?" exclaimed the giant. "And what would a gent of your size be doing in a place like Kirby Crossing, I'd like to know?"

"I'm a lot smaller than you are, Harry," said Silver.

"Across the shoulder, maybe, but not across the brain," said the big man cheerfully. "It would sprain Kirby Crossing in the small of the back and both ankles, to have a gent of your size of name inside of it, man!"

"I'm not wearing the same name," answered Silver. "I'm a Mexican, when I go in there."

"Hold on!" cried One-eyed Harry. "You mean that you're a bare-footed greaser in rags, like you were when I first seen you, Silver?"

"That's it. Something like that."

Harry grinned. "What's the little game in the wind now?" he asked.

"Would you help me?" asked Silver curiously.

"Me? And why not? Sure I'd help you. And how?"

"By being my boss," said Silver, "and letting me drive that mule into town for you, as though it were my job."

The mirth of One-eyed Harry thundered through the air like a roaring cataract in a narrow valley. "Me with a servant?" he said. "Me with Silver for a servant? And why not? But hold on, Jim Silver!"

"Well?" said Silver.

"There's another way of lookin' at these things. What kind of hurricane are you goin' to raise when you get into Kirby Crossing? And after you raise it, how you goin' to ride it? Have I gotta sit on top of the same kind of a wind that you like?"

Silver smiled. "I don't know what's ahead of me," he declared.

"Something like Barry Christian and his thugs?" asked One-eyed Harry.

"I hope not."

"No," said the big man, "it ain't likely that you'll ever crash into anything as tough as Barry Christian, if you live to be a thousand. They ain't hung Barry yet. You know that?"

The face of Silver darkened. "I know that," he agreed.

"And it doesn't seem likely to me," added One-eyed Harry Bench, "that they ever *will* hang him, because it don't seem likely that the rope was ever braided or wove that'll hang a neck like his. But about the things you're after in Kirby Crossing—tell me, Jim Silver— ain't it a blood trail?"

"Why do you ask that?" said Silver, frowning.

"Because," answered Bench, "I've heard more'n one gent say that you never ride on no trail at all unless it's a blood trail? Is that true?"

"I hope not," answered Silver. "I hope I'm not such a devil as that, Harry."

"Well," answered Bench, "there's a good many men have seen you at work here and there, and they all say that they never hear of a trail of yours that wasn't spotted with red before the end of it. Is there a killing in your mind, in Kirby Crossing?"

"There is!" said Silver, suddenly and grimly. "And you can count yourself out of the party, Harry. It may be more than you'll want to swallow."

"A mean gent that you're after?" said Bench wistfully.

"A man whose face I wouldn't know," said Silver.

"Not know?" cried Bench. He groaned with curiosity. Then he exclaimed: "Ah, well, I can't live forever. I'm goin' to be a fool for once more in my life. Count me in, Jim. I'll stay as long as I can!"

Chapter IX

KIRBY CROSSING

THEY expected to get into the town that night, but when they reached the place they found that Kirby Crossing was no crossing at all, for the bridge had gone down in the flood that was still roaring through the ravine. Disappointed teamsters were piling up on the two sides of the stream, waiting until the bridge could be built again, and helping earnestly in its construction. It would be another week before the flimsy structure could span the creek, though the big stone foundation for the central pier was still in place and undamaged, and though the biggest trees were being felled and dragged down to build the understructure of the bridge.

The only other way of getting over Kirby Creek was to go nearly another fifty miles up Kirby Run, and then come down it on the farther side of the stream, after reaching the ford. However, that ford was only practical for men and horses, and active men and horses at that.

Silver and big One-eyed Harry camped for the night opposite the little mining town, and then went upstream the next morning. It was nearly sunset of the third day before they got into the place. A strange outfit they were, and no one had a glance for anything other than One-eyed Harry. His picturesqueness took all glances away from the big-shouldered, long-shanked Mexican who trotted along bareheaded, a mop of shaggy black hair falling down over his forehead, as he led on a shambling mule and a chestnut stallion that looked fit for riding, but which carried nothing but a big pack saddle.

The big horse had the legs and the look of speed, if one cared to examine closely; but it was covered with dust and had a very sad limp in a foreleg. Not a man in all of Kirby Crossing but would have laughed if he were told that this was that famous outlaw stallion, Parade, which had defied capture so long and caused such a wastage of money in the hunt for him that at last he became known as the hundred-thousand-dollar horse. It was too incredible.

The little group paused in Kirby Crossing only long enough to buy flour, bacon, a few canned goods, and get the latest papers. But the newspapers were far less important than the word that ran from lip to lip.

The State penitentiary, hardly eighty miles away, had been the scene of a cunning escape. One David Holman, then lodged in the death house, had cut through the bars of his cell, gained the prison yard, and climbed over the guard wall by the aid of a ladder of silk equipped with fine aluminum grapples at one end. Finally he either had drowned in the lake in the middle of which the penitentiary stood, or else had swum the long distance to the shore on a night when a veritable hurricane was blowing. Only one thing was certain—that some of the guards must have been bribed to look the other way. But so far the investigation had convicted no one of guilt.

It was One-eyed Harry who spent an hour or more buying the food and getting the gossip. Silver, in the meantime was slipping along securely in his Mexican disguise from group to group and from window to window, until at last he had peeked into every saloon, and examined the people in the dining room of the hotel, and in the restaurant. He was searching for a man with a peculiar birdlike alertness of head and manner, and a singular lightness of step. Or if the man could not be found, he hoped to get a glimpse, perhaps, of Edith Alton Kenyon.

But he was disappointed. He had to rejoin One-eyed

Harry, who, in the presence of a few yawning spectators, cursed him as a lazy greaser for being late, and threatened to flay him alive if he were ever tardy again.

Then they went up the valley, and camped between the edge of Kirby Run and the trees that crowded the valley. They chose the site of some old diggings. Gold was everywhere in the sands of the creek. The only trouble was that it was scarce, and there were few places where a man could wash a day's wages with any ease. However, One-eyed Harry Bench was willing to stay there as long as Silver needed him.

"If it hadn't been for you routing me out with a bullet," said Bench, "I'd still be out there in the dessert, eating sand with my bacon and hating the whole world! I'll camp anywhere you say. And what could be better than this here?"

It was a good camp, in fact, with plenty of food and water, and a view of big mountains before them and behind. Kirby Crossing was only a little over a mile away.

They built a lean-to the next morning, and Silver left his friend arranging the stones for an outdoor fireplace, while he slipped up into the town again. There were other Mexicans in the town, and one saloon at the end of the street was their gathering place. Into the brown horde. Silver went, to let his disguise be thoroughly tested. But he had few doubts that it would pass muster; a dozen times he had used it in old Mexico itself.

In the saloon he kept his eyes down and his ears open, while he drank tequila. But he heard nothing that had any bearing on his quest. There was only talk and more talk about the prison break. It pleased the Mexicans to know that the government and the law had failed. Their rattling voices rose to crescendos; they laughed heartily, flashing their eyes at one another.

But what was the prison break to Silver? He left the saloon and resumed his search through the town. His eye was so trained that half a second's pause in front of a window could show him all the faces inside. And a few side glances were enough for his study of whole groups as he passed among them. But he had worked up and down the street twice before some one caught his eye.

It was a man he had seen before, seated in the back room of a saloon, playing poker and chewing nervously at a cigar. But only when he walked out onto the street did the attention of Silver fall seriously on him. For he had a quick, lightly rising step, like that of a sprinter in the pink of condition for a race. As he walked, his head had the same birdlike alertness that Silver had noted in the unknown companion of Edith Alton, that morning in the ravine. The farther the man drew into the distance, the more convinced was Silver that he had found his quarry.

A warm little glow ran through him. He had to set his teeth to keep from laughing aloud.

The stranger mounted a horse tethered in front of the saloon, and rode out of town at a dogtrot that freshened to a lope as he gained the open beyond. But Silver was not far behind. He kept among the trees that bordered the narrow road closely on either side, and his long legs flew over the ground with the easy stride of a natural runner.

He had a chance to note several things on the way. The first was that he was behind a good horseman. The second was that the stranger was by no means used to the Western style of riding. And finally his conviction was that in spite of the cow-puncher outfit, time-rubbed as it was, his quarry was quite a stranger to the West and Western ways.

He was inclined to take the reins in both hands, for instance, instead of reining across the neck. And when they came to a runlet that ran across the road, the rider pitched forward in the saddle and hunched over, as though expecting the mustang to jump the barrier. Instead, being Western, that cow pony calmly trotted through the water.

It was not a long run. In twenty minutes or less the rider turned off toward the creek, and halted in front of an old, disused cabin, on the front of which a flap of canvas had been hung to take the place of a door. A burly young Mexican with a mustache that glistened like black glass came to take the horse of his master, throwing down the ax with which he had been chopping wood.

The rider disappeared into the cabin, while Silver sat on the edge of the woods and watched the Mexican put up the pony in a lean-to that was attached to the end of the cabin. This was only until saddle and bridle had been removed, and hobbles fitted. After that the mustang was turned loose to graze on the good grass.

When this had been done, the Mexican returned to his ax. Silver, who was now breathing easily again, came out from the trees and stood to watch. The other gave him a wave of the hand, and then went on with his swinging of the ax.

"There is no chance to talk, amigo," said he. "That gringo has the eye of a hawk and the ear of a grizzly bear. He keeps me working all day. Except for the good pay, I am only a slave. If you have something to say to me, wait for me to-night in the saloon in Kirby Crossing, where all of our people meet."

"The fact is," said Silver, "that this work is too hard for you, friend. It needs a stronger man."

"A stronger man?" said the Mexican, scowling. "Who sent you out here to trouble me?"

"I came of my own accord," said Silver. "I have a kind heart. I never want to see a man working beyond his strength."

"You, perhaps," said the Mexican, "could do this work very easily?"

"No doubt," said Silver.

"You could cut the wood, do the cooking, wash some gold out of the creek sands? You could wash the soiled clothes and sweep out the cabin, and then find spare time to shoot fresh meat for his table?"

"I could do all of those things," said Silver. "What's more, I *shall* to them."

The Mexican stared. Then his eyes glassed over with

rage. His chest swelled, his chin sank. "Fool of a stone-faced half-wit!" he roared. "Get out before I cut you in two with the ax!"

"Don't lift the ax," said Silver, "or I'll have to take it away from you."

A voice spoke suddenly, sharply, from the cabin doorway, and there was the master of the house.

"What's the matter out there, José." asked he.

"Matter, Señor Lorens?" said José. "Here is a crazy man who says that this work is too hard for me, and that he is going to take my place!"

Silver turned to Lorens and gave him a deep bow.

"A bright day to you, señor," said Silver. "May the sunshine fall on your heart; may the gold gather for you in the sands."

This flowery outburst, in swift Mexican, set Lorens chuckling.

"This fellow is a poet, and poets are the devil, José," said he. "Does he say that he is going to take your place?"

"He may be a devil," said José, grating his teeth together, "but even a devil will feel the edge of this ax."

He gave it a swing as he spoke.

"What's your name?" asked Lorens.

"Juan," said Silver.

"Juan, I like the look of you," said Lorens. "Your hair might be mowed or tied back from your eyes, but you look able to do something."

"I can do everything that that man can do, and then twist his neck," said Silver.

"Do you hear, Señor Lorens?" said José, trembling with rage. "This is one of those fools who boasts and thinks that his loud talking will be the thing that weakens the heart of another man! Away with you, you lying, stealing, ragged thief! Would an honest man wear such clothes? Look, señor! His trousers are not long enough to reach his ankles, and therefore he keeps them rolled up to his knees. There is nothing on his body but that cheap shirt. See the sandals on his feet! Señor, let me send him on his travels again!"

"If you can," said Lorens calmly. "Drive him as far as you please—if you're able!"

Chapter X

A MAN OF TALENTS

Jose, when he had received this permission, gaped at Silver with a sudden joy. Then, weighing the broad-bladed ax in both hands, he advanced at him with short, quick steps, like a boxer.

"Hold on!" called Lorens. "An ax against a man with empty hands?"

"Señor," said Silver, "I have a knife, but I shall not use it. Who will use weapons on children, señor?"

José uttered a short howl, something like that of a dog when it starts to bay the moon. Then he came with a skip and a leap and a swing of the ax right at Silver.

In José there was no such folly as would lead him to try a downright blow that might be side-stepped. Instead, he feinted at the head, and then swept the ax around in a mighty circle. The edge of the blade flamed with keenness. It could have cloven deep into the body of Silver if it struck fairly home. Instead, it merely brushed through the top hair of his black wig as it swished by, for he had crouched suddenly close to the earth. The weight of the stroke turned José half around. He knew that he had missed, and that his failure was apt to be his ruin. Even while his arms were carrying his body around, his head turned toward Silver, and his face was desperate. But there was nothing that he could do. The blow that found him had the weight of Silver leaning straight behind it. José fell in a heap.

Silver took the ax from those numb hands and swayed it lightly into the air.

"This poor rascal," said Silver, "may come back to

steal, señor. But If I tap him across the back of the neck until the bone snaps, then I can weight him with stones and drop him into the river. With this current he will soon be rolled to bits. In five days, if they have dragged the river, they would be able to find no more than a finger bone of all of him."

Lorens began to laugh heartily. He was a handsome fellow, a little too thin of face, a little too bright and active of eye; now he was alight with appreciation.

"Don't kill the poor rat, Juan," said he. "Do you think he'll come back if you tell him that you don't want him around?"

"I must talk to him in a special way," said Silver. "Permit me, señor, and his face shall never be seen around here again!"

"Talk to him any way you please," said Lorens. "I have an idea that you're going to work for me, Juan."

"Ah, señor," said Silver, "to hear you say that is already as good as roast kid and frijoles in my stomach. Hey! José!"

José, coming to his senses by degrees, was startled by this cry to his feet. He stood wavering, looking wildly from Silver to his master.

"The honorable and rich señor," said Silver, "is tired of wasting his money, tired of spending the kindness of his heart on a poor thickwit, a wretched fellow who knows nothing of cooking, who leaves the floor of the house dirty, who has no luck in finding gold, and who cannot make the smoke of the fire blow away from the house. He sends you away, José. And he tells you that if you are seen near this house again, to beg or to steal, he will make you disappear—like this!"

At that he picked up a small stone from the ground, hurled it far into the air and when it spun, hovering, at the height of its rise, he flashed a revolver into his hand and fired. The glimmering stone and the bullet met with an audible impact, and the stone disappeared.

José still was blinking in the direction of that spot where the little rock had hung in the air. Now his mouth opened slowly.

He had seen something that was worth more to him than a thousand hours of explanation and lecturing. He backed up a few steps, turned, and fled dodging, like a snipe when it goes winging against the wind to avoid the gun of the hunter.

"You see, señor," said Silver, "that when we deal with children, we do not need weapons except to frighten the silly fools!"

"Juan, you speak good Spanish," said Lorens, standing in the doorway, with his chin on his fist and study in his eyes.

"I learned it, my master," said Silver, "in Mexico City itself. I was in service there."

"What sort of service?"

"Shining silver, and taking the small dogs out for their walks."

Lorens smiled, but there was still dubious thought in his eyes.

"How do you wear that revolver?"

"Here under my left arm," said Silver. "Most people don't expect it to come from that place. So I have a chance to surprise them, and to please myself, and that means that everybody is happy."

"Or dead," suggested Lorens.

"Or dead, señor," said Silver, bowing.

"A fellow with your talents," said Lorens, "ought never have to work with his hands."

"Observe my palms," answered Silver. "They are smoother than the hands of a young maiden, señor."

"Ah?" said Lorens. "They why are you taking a job here with me?"

"I am not in my own country, where I would be known," said Silver. "If I were there, señor, there are villages where the men would stop everything the instant that I appear, and the women, without being bidden, would at once begin to cook. One would roast a kid. Another would seethe a chicken. Another old woman would bring out her finest cheese, packed in wet salt grass, delicious in the mouth with wine. I should sit, señor, in front of the fonda, and drink with the head men of the town, and then eat, and ask one or two of the notables to sit down with me and taste my food. And when I had finished eating, I should pay them all ten times over by telling them three true stories of three days of my life. They would give me their blessing, follow me to the edge of the town, fill my saddlebags with food, press a canteen of good red wine into my hands, place a little bottle of tequila in my coat pocket, and tell me to hurry back to them again!"

He delivered this long speech with a sort of lordly flourish.

"Well," said Lorens, "Mexico is still in the old place. Why aren't you there?"

"Because all of my countrymen are not so kind and so true," said Silver. "There are some rude fellows that you may have heard of."

"The rurales, perhaps?"

"The señor," said Silver, "sees at a glance to the heart of everything. The rurales know that there is a price on my head. Therefore they hunt me with more passion, señor, than the Americanos of your country will hunt a wild duck—though they may have plenty of tame ducks waddling about in their back yards!"

Lorens laughed again, but very shortly. "Look here, Juan," he said. "You won't want to be working for me very long as a cook and a hunter and a fire tender."

"Señor," said Silver, "you will not very long be camped by this river, pretending to hunt for gold. And before you leave this place, you may have found better ways to employ me."

"What do you mean by saying that I only pretend to hunt for gold?" asked Lorens.

"What do I mean? Nothing! If the señor is angry, I mean nothing. I know that the señor has eyes enough for two, and ears enough for two, also, and a tongue that is capable of speaking for all his affairs."

"No, but tell me why you think I only pretend to look for gold?"

"Because I saw you playing poker, señor. And after I had watched you shuffle the deck three times, I knew that you could dig more money out of the hands of men with a pack of cards than strong miners can earn by digging and blasting at a mountain of rock all their lives!"

Lorens tapped his rapid, slender fingers against his lips, looking over his knuckles at Silver critically.

"Juan," said he, "you're an impudent rascal, and you see too much."

"It is true," said Silver calmly. "The señor does not want a blind José, but a Juan with two eyes, perhaps. Yet if you tell me to close them, I am blind."

"I know what you mean," remarked Lorens. "You're able to see anything and remember only what I want you to know."

"The señor understands," said Silver.

"Juan, you have killed men in your time."

"I have had that joy, señor," said Silver. "I have seen the faces of my enemies turn black under my hands."

Lorens shrugged his shoulders as though to get rid of a feeling of cold up his spine.

"What money do you want?" he asked. "How will you have it?"

"I shall be paid according to my services," said Silver. "If it is to cook and clean and hunt for the señor, the scraps of food that are left will be food and pay for me. But if more important matters come, and they are put in my hands, then the señor himself will know how to reward me. It is not for money alone that I work, but for pleasure, señor, and to fill my hands with the name of a man!"

This speech seemed to please Lorens more than all the rest put together.

"You're a hard bit of steel, Juan," said he. "You'll take an edge and keep it. I want to know one thing from you. Did you ever hear of a man named Silver— an American?"

"The Señor Silver?" said Silver, looking down. "I have heard of him and seen him."

"Tell me what sort of a man he is?"

"A man to beware of. He has done certain things.

He shoots very straight, and he shoots very quickly. And he has killed men, señor—a great many of them."

"A fellow like that, Juan—a fellow who answers the very description of this man Silver, may be on my trail. I don't know. I'm not sure that he will follow me. But he's one that I should like you to have in mind. Dream of him as he was, Juan. Look for him in the shadow under every tree. Listen for his voice. Watch for the flash of his gun!"

"He shall be more in my mind than my own self," said Silver.

"Tell me this," said Lorens. "Would you stand up to a fellow like Silvertip, do you think?"

"Perhaps he is a larger man than I am." said Silver. "But I should hope to stand up to him. A brown hand can be as quick as a white one, and a white skin does not turn bullets."

"Juan," said Lorens seriously, "you and I are going to get on together. You don't need to make a slave of yourself. If you can shoot fresh meat and cook it, that will be enough for me, along with some coffee. And I suppose you know how to cook frijoles?"

"You shall be glad I am with you," said Silver, "every time you eat the food I cook."

He bowed again, and, looking up through the overhanging shag of his forelock, he studied the face of the man who within this week had sent a rifle bullet inches from his head. There was murder in that thin, handsome face. There were infinite possibilities of treachery in the uncertain brightness of the eyes. And behind all, there was a quick flame of intelligence. If he were to pull the wool over these eyes continually, Silver knew that he would have to be on guard constantly. He would have to live like a dog with a wolf, never knowing when the teeth would be in his throat.

But behind this man, somehow and somewhere, loomed the form of the girl. Perhaps it was in the handwriting of Lorens that the words had been written: "—out fail in Kirby Cr—" And perhaps through this man, also, Silver could come in touch with him who had encompassed the death of Buck, and whose name began with "Nel—"

Danger breathed now out of the very air, but opportunity was in it, also.

Chapter XI

THE REWARD POSTER

Luck favored Silver in the execution of his first domestic duties for Lorens. He took the rifle of Lorens, a beautiful weapon, and walked ten minutes, straight through the woods, when a stag sprang out of a covert hardly twenty yards from him. Silver let it run until his bead was perfect, and then sank the bullet behind the shoulder.

The stag was young, but when all the less choice parts were discarded, there remained more than two hundred pounds of good, edible meat. Silver loaded himself with half of it and brought it close to the shack of Lorens. He went back and got the other half. After resting, he put the whole crushing burden on his shoulders. He stepped out from among the trees and came up to the shack with a swinging stride.

Lorens was sitting cross-legged under a tree, smoking a pipe. He sprang up with an exclamation.

"Venison, man? Venison, Juan?"

"It is not veal," said Silver, putting down the load.

"That's something José could never get for me," said Lorens. "He said that the deer were all frightened out of the valley, long ago."

"You know, señor," said Silver, "that we never find what we do not hope for. But I, Juan, will keep you in venison."

"There's enough there for a whole camp!" exclaimed Lorens.

He tried to pick up the burden, and it slipped out of his straining hands.

"Great guns!" said Lorens under his breath, and

73

with profound awe stared at Silver askance. He had heard the rifle crack in the far distance; he had seen his new man come swinging in with a light, long stride, carrying that weight and hardly breathing under it. He began to look now at the lean shanks of Silver.

"Some men are different," Silver heard him mutter. "The way mules are smaller and stronger than horses, or cats are stronger than dogs!"

On venison steaks broiled to crust outside and of a melting tenderness within, they dined that night, with potatoes fried crisp, and cress from the edge of the running water, and thick, strong black coffee. And Lorens declared that he had not properly eaten since he had left—

The name of the city remained unspoken, but Silver did not think it would be hard to fit in the name of the metropolis where this gambler had been plying his trade. For all his good looks, the man had the manner and something of the look of a rat that had lived underground most of its days.

He said, as they sipped coffee—Silver sitting farther from the fire than his employer as though out of respect, but in reality because he wished to have his face studied as little as possible: "Juan, tell me something of your old life down there in Mexico, will you?"

Silver pretended a distress which was not altogether unreal. Then he said: "Ask me for my blood, señor, but do not ask me for my past. The old days are rope that is made; the new days are rope that is in the winding; my past may not please you, but the new rope may be what you want."

"For hanging myself?" asked Lorens.

The question was so apt that Silver started, but Lorens was already laughing at his own remark.

"You're right, Juan," said Lorens. "The fellow who talks about his past is not likely to have much of a future. Here's a poor devil who's had a past, I suppose. A batch of these posters came to town to-day. Fast work on the printing press, eh?"

He put on the ground before Silver a picture of a

man of not more than thirty, with a strong, dignified, even a refined face, with every capacity of thought and feeling indicated in it. But the big print offered a reward of five thousand dollars for the apprehension of this man dead or alive. The name was David Holman, and Silver remembered hearing that this was the criminal who had recently broken out of the penitentiary, less than a hundred miles away.

"What d'you think of that face?" asked Lorens.

"He is too strong to be only a little good, or a little bad," said Silver. "He must be everything or nothing."

Lorens picked up the poster, and looked from it suddenly and piercingly at Silver.

"You're no fool, Juan," he said.

Then he added, half to himself: "Dead or alive! Dead of alive! Think of that! These fellows around here will hunt for a week, every day, for the sake of bagging a timber wolf that only has a ten-dollar bounty on his scalp. Dead or alive, and five thousand dollars for the lucky fellow who draws a dead bead and pulls the trigger! Eh, Juan?" he said, making his voice suddenly cheerful. "That would be a handsome bit of money to have down yonder in Mexico, where things are cheaper!"

Silver shook his head with real distaste.

"Blood money, señor!" said he. "I have killed men, but never for money."

"No?" said Lorens.

"No," said Silver. "Never for money. And I never shall."

"But five thousand dollars! That's a fortune!"

"It would all taste of blood!" said Silver.

Lorens began to brood again, the lower part of his face propped up in the flat of his hand, and his eyes lifting suddenly, now and again, to his companion. At last he said: "Juan, I have to be in two places at once to-night."

"Yes, señor," said Silver.

"One place is in Kirby Crossing. One is right here in this camp. Understand?"

"A man's body cannot be in two places at once," said Silver.

"One of me will have to be you."

"Yes, señor."

"Juan, I've known you only for a few hours, but I'm going to trust you. I want you to go into Kirby Crossing and at ten o'clock stand across the street from the hotel. You hear me? At ten o'clock. And stay there the rest of the night if you have to. Can you do that without closing your eyes?"

"Once," said Silver dreamily, "for four days there were men around a little nest of rocks. If I so much as nodded, they knew it, and crawled closer."

Lorens grinned, a quick contortion of the face that became still again at once.

"As you wait there," said Lorens, "two or three times an hour you'll be smoking a cigarette."

"Yes, señor."

"Well, then, every time you light a cigarette, take two matches under your finger and scratch them both—so that the two will burn at the same time."

"I hear you, señor."

"After a time—I don't know when—I think that a woman will come up to you. She will ask for Charlie. You'll tell her that you come in his name."

"Does she speak Spanish, señor?"

"Enough to understand that."

"How shall I know that she is the right woman?"

"If she's young, pretty, and holds her head high, with her chin up a bit, you'll know that she's the right one."

"I understand," said Silver, his heart beginning to beat fast. For who could it be except Edith Alton Kenyon, that cunning trickster? And he wished, in a sudden moment of savage rage, that poor Ned Kenyon could be sitting here to listen to the words from Lorens.

"You can go now," said Lorens. "Buy two horses and two saddles. How much will they cost—two mighty good ones?"

"Five hundred dollars apiece," said Silver.

Lorens grunted. "That's worse than blood money. I mean something around a hundred and fifty dollars."

"It can be done, señor. There are horses for gentlemen and there are horses for Juan. I shall buy two horses for Juan."

"That's it. Put the girl on one of 'em, and bring her out here."

He took out a wallet and counted the money, while Silver scowled at the fire. He liked this very little. The man was, in fact, trusting him. And to betray the trust even of a fellow who had tried to put a bullet through his head, went sore against the grain.

"Here's four hundred," said Lorens. "And that's a lot of money for me just now. Do your best with it."

"I shall bring a hundred dollars back," said Silver, "and still you'll be satisfied."

"I don't want a hundred back. Spend all of it. Or if you can satisfy me with less, put the change in your pocket. You can go now. Buy the horses, and be opposite the hotel at ten o'clock, ready to wait there until the morning, if it should so happen you have to."

"In all things, as you please, señor," said Silver.

He took the money and counted it, and rose to his feet.

"One more thing," cautioned Lorens harshly. "I'm giving you enough money to tempt you a little, perhaps. But you remember this: You've been a big man in your own country, but you're not a big man in this one. And if you try to run out on me, I'll have the scalp off your head and the marrow out of your bones—I'll have it, and there are plenty who'll help me to get it!"

His thin face wrinkled like an old leaf with sudden malice as the mere thought of his promised vengeance passed through his mind.

"Señor," said Silver, "only a fool promises. A wise man waits to have judgment passed on his deeds."

"All right, all right," muttered Lorens. "You sound like a copy book. I'll see what you bring home to me from Kirby Crossing!"

Chapter XII

SILVER'S GAME

SILVER went back to Kirby Crossing on the run. He only slackened his pace to walk with his long stride through the town, and he lingered an instant to watch the strange spectacle of the building of a bridge by night, for the work was being pressed twenty-four hours a day. Lanterns hung in a long festoon over the timbers. The great underlogs were being wedged and bound in place, and the bridge began to look like a skeleton of what it would finally appear.

Silver went on past it. He entered the dark of the open country in the lower part of the valley, and here he sprang again into his Indian trot that shifted the ground rapidly behind him. When he was not far from the lean-to which he and One-eyed Harry had put on, he whistled. And from the dark of the brush sprang Parade, and came racing, with a whinny.

He went round and round Silver like a bird in the air about to settle on a nest. He was dancing and snorting, with the hand of his master on his shoulder, when big Harry Bench came out of the lean-to. In the dark he looked more gigantic than ever.

"Silver?" he called. "Man, man, that hoss has been about crazy while you was away. He's come smelling around the shack, and he's still-hunted your trail down the valley. Where you been, brother?"

Silver went into the lean-to and sat on a homemade stool in the corner. The stallion stood with head and shoulders intruding through the doorway.

"I'm up the valley on the other side of the Crossing," said Silver. "Take a look at me! I'm Juan,

78

the greaser, who works for a fellow named Lorens. I've got two minutes to spend here, and no more than that. I have to get back. I'm working for a fellow with an eye like a hawk and the wit of a prairie coyote. One day, when I was wearing a white skin, this same Lorens put a bullet inches from my ear and then ran out on me. Just now he doesn't know me, but if he guesses that I'm lying to him, or that my skin is not as dark as it seems to be, he'll take the first good chance to shoot me in the back."

"What in the nation do you wanta waste your time on him, then?" said One-eyed Harry, lifting his huge voice.

"Because," said Silver, "I'm on the outside edge of a regular whirlpool, old-timer. Lorens is the edge of the whirl, and if I stick to him, I think I may be drawn into the middle of the pool."

"And who the devil wants to be drowned in a whirlpool?" demanded Harry, staring.

"Call it a dance instead of a whirlpool," said Silver, "and all of the dancers wear knives, and I'm blindfolded, and I never know what tune they'll strike up next, or where they'll step. But there's a lying crook of a woman, a murderer, and somebody who's tried to murder *me*. They're all elements in the job, and I don't know how many other forces are behind 'em. You can see that it's a pretty picture, Harry!"

"You like it!" exclaimed One-eyed Harry Bench. "Doggone me if you don't like it a lot. Kind of makes your eye shine just to think of that dance, eh? That kind of a job is just like pork and beans to you, ain't it?"

"Like it?" said Silver, surprised. "Of course I don't like it. I'm likely to lose my hide any minute, and my head along with it."

"You like it," said Harry Bench, pointing with his huge, grimy hand. "That's the game for you, the way poker is the game for the small-time gambler. You ain't happy, by thunder, unless your life is on the table as the stakes."

He took a step toward Silver and shook his hand at him. A sort of horrified realization came over that rugged face as Bench said:

"You're goin' to keep after them, you're goin' to keep playin' that game till you're killed. You know that, Silver? You're goin' to play with the fire till you're burned to the bone. What makes you such a fool? You can't keep ten knives in the air all your life. One of 'em is bound to fall sometime and stick right into your heart. Hear me talk?"

"Hear you?" said Silver, apparently irritated. "Of course I hear you, and you're talking like a half-wit, Harry. I'm not up there with that tiger cat, Lorens, for pleasure. I'm up there because there's a crooked game in the wind, and because a friend of mine has suffered on account of it already. That's why I'm there!"

"If you're not in that mess, you're in another one. It's always the frying pan or the fire for you, Silver!"

Silver started to deny the charge, but as he parted his lips to speak, his glance went inward upon his life and showed him the crowded story of his past in such pictures that he was suddenly mute. It was true. All of his days he had played with fire. He could tell himself that he was simply following the courses which chance led him into, but why was it that every trail he put his feet on was a trail of danger?

So he was mute for an instant, seeing those pictures, and out of the past reading the future. For what big Harry Bench had said was indubitably true. No man could continue to play with fire without being finally burned to an ash.

Gradually he drew himself out of the dark humor and scowled up at One-eyed Harry. Bench was pacing back and forth, taking the breadth of the little room in three strides, and whirling on his heel and toe. For all the size and the bulk of that man, he was as active as a big cat. Silver vaguely admired the magnificence of that physique, so swift and yet so massive. He himself had the strength of two men in his arms, but he knew that in the grasp of this giant he would crumble like sand.

"Somebody has oughta watch out after you," said Bench. "There had oughta be friends to keep you hobbled. Even your hoss has to stay and worry about you!"

Silver looked toward the sooty muzzle, the beautiful, deerlike eye of the stallion, and smiled. "Harry," said Silver, "maybe there's a lot in what you say. The more I think about it, the more I agree with you. I've got to stop my crazy ways. And I'm going to do it. Believe me, partner? This is the last job that I take over on my hands, no matter how the luck tries to drag me into trouble."

"Sure!" growled Harry Bench. "That's what you say now. But you'll be changing your mind one of these days. If you got sense, you'll stay here and let Lorens go hang."

"He won't go hang, and I want the job of the hanging," said Silver. "If I don't hang him myself, I want to point him out to the hangman, and turn him over with his hands tied behind his back, if he's the sort that I think I can prove he is! Now stop talking about me. I want to ask you a question."

"Fire away."

"There's a fellow named David Holman—"

"That just escaped from the death house at the prison. Yeah. I know about that."

"I've an idea that my friend, Lorens, up the valley, has a sort of an interest in Mr. Holman. What put Holman in the death house? What did he do?"

"Oh, nothin' much," said One-eyed Harry. "He come out from the East to be a cashier in a bank over in Tuckaway. Pickin' up experience, you see? But he wanted to pick up some hard cash, too. And he took it out of the vaults. After a while he was pretty far in the hole, and so this here Holman, he planned to have the bank robbed, and, of course, the robbery would cover up what he'd stole.

"So he got a pair of yeggs to work with him, and one night him and them robbed the bank, all right. But it happened that Sheriff Bert Philips was riding back into town that night, after chasin' a half-breed hoss thief a coupla hundred miles and never sighting him. And he seen three men sneakin' out from the rear of the bank, and he hollered out to them. They ducked away to their horses and run for it. He followed and yelled for help, and some gents who were havin' a late night of it at a saloon, they come out and joined in the chase. And then there was a long run, and the three of 'em got away for the time being.

"But the chase was so long that this here Dave Holman didn't have a chance to fill in his plan, which was to be back in his home in bed when the day begun, with his split of the stag stowed away somewhere safe. He was still on the run at sunup. And then he says to himself, that as long as he's goin' to be found out, he'd better be caught for a sheep then for just a lamb. So he ups and murders them two gents, and takes their share of the loot, and lights out with it. And the sheriff and his posse comes along while there's still a spark of life in one of the dyin' gents, and this feller tells about the holdup, and how Holman had planned it, and how Holman had murdered them. And the sheriff, he follers on, and gets a sight of Holman on a dead-beat horse, and runs him down and hauls him in.

"When it comes to the trial, this here Holman, he puts up a cock-and-bull story about how the two thugs had come to his house in the middle of the night and forced him at the point of a gun to go to the bank with 'em and open the safe, and how they'd kept him under their guns, and made him run with 'em, and how he'd taken the first chance to get hold of a revolver and shoot the pair of 'em. And why did he run when the sheriff came up after him? Well, it was because all of the swag was on him, and he seen that it would be hard to explain things away and prove that he was an honest man. It was a pretty far-fetched story, and the whole jury, it busted out laughin' in the middle of the yarn, they say. So they made him guilty of murder, and there you are!"

Silver had listened attentively to this story, and now he nodded his head. "What that has to do with Lorens," he said, "I don't know. But Lorens has a lot of interest in that fellow Holman, I think. Now, Harry, there's one thing more for me to say to you. I'm going back up the valley. I'm going to be in Kirby Crossing for a while, and then I'm going on. Every day I'm going to try to get in touch with you. If I don't manage that, I want you to start on the trail for me, because it may be that I'll be needing help. Will you do that?"

"I'll do it glad and willing," answered One-eyed Harry. "You're going back into the fire, are you?"

"This one job is the last one, but I've got to finish it," said Silver uneasily.

He stood up.

"Try to keep people away from Parade," he cautioned. "There are more men who know that horse than there are who know me. And if Parade is spotted, people will know that I'm not far away—and that will complicate everything. This disguise business is thin ice to skate on, and it won't take much to make me break through. I'll put Parade in the woods, and he'll stay there till I come back. Just see that he has water and grain. And so long, Harry."

Harry followed his friend out into the night.

"I hate to have you go, partner," said he. "It seems to me that there's a lot of trouble pilin' up in the air around us."

"Perhaps there is," said Silver. "But this is the last time for me, Harry."

"The last time you hunt trouble?" echoed Harry. "You couldn't stay away from it. No more than a dope fiend can stay away from his dope. But so long, Jim. Will that hoss stay there without no hobbles, even?"

They stood together in the dark of the trees near the lean-to, and Silver spoke to the horse and patted the silk of the neck.

"He'll stay here till he hears me call or whistle," said he, "I think he'd stay here if the brush were set on fire.

But your job, old son, is to keep people away from this neck of the woods during the day. Mind you, if anybody puts an eye on the horse, I'm next door to a gone goose!"

Chapter XIII

PERRY NELLIHAN

SILVER ran back to Kirby Crossing and went to the biggest horse dealer's yard. It was out on the edge of the town—a little shack of a house, a sprawling shed, and a tangle of corral fences all within sound of the flowing of the river. The proprietor was eating his supper alone in his kitchen when Silver tapped at the open door and saw a face swollen with fat and red-stained by whisky lifted from a platter of jumbled food.

"How much of a pair of hosses do you want?" asked the dealer sharply.

"Four hundred dollars' worth," said Silver simply. "Horses and saddles."

The dealer ducked his head and coughed to cover his grin of satisfaction. Five minutes later Silver sat on his heels with his back against a corral fence, and watched a wrangler run half a dozen horses into the lantern light of the inclosure.

"No, señor," said Silver. "It is not four hundred dollars' worth of horse meat that I want, but two horses at two hundred dollars apiece."

"Here!" exclaimed the dealer. "There ain't a pair of this lot that ain't worth two hundred bucks."

But though he blustered, he realized that he was not dealing with a fool. He brought in new selections. It was not until twenty animals had been brought before him that Silver elected to try one. He took the one he tried. And twenty more went before him before he selected its mate. Then he had a good gray and a roan. Neither of them was a picture horse, but each promised to be full of service. It rather amused Silver to

85

note that he was using his best endeavors for Lorens, who would eventually be his open enemy. But the instinct of the bargainer had control of him.

By the time the horses were secured, the dealer lifted his lantern and shone the light of it into the eyes of Silver.

"If everybody bought hosses like you do, stranger," said he, "I'd have to go out of business or turn myself into an honest man!"

Silver took the horses with the flimsy, battered equipment that was included in the sale price, and led the pair to the long hitch rack in front of the hotel.

It was nearly ten o'clock, so he went to his designated post opposite the hotel and sat down on his heels again, with his back leaned against a wall.

There were few people in the street. Only about the doors of the saloons appeared the forms of men entering or slipping away. Those lighted doors seemed to be attracting the inhabitants as lamps attract insects on a summer night. But most of the houses down the street were already darkened, because the town dwellers of a small Western community retire early and begin the day betimes. Even in the hotel, only three windows above the ground floor were lighted. And at ten o'clock the veranda was empty, and the hanging lanterns that illumined it were put out.

Silver stood up, stretched his cramped legs, and settled down on his heels again. He was perfectly content. Sometimes invisible whirlpools of dust brushed against him, and the taste of alkali came into his mouth. But in his nostrils there was the fragrance of adventure, and the light in his mind was more than lamps could shed.

The minutes went by him like stealthy feet. It was eleven, or close to that hour. Only a single window in the facade of the hotel was lamplighted. One of the saloons had closed for the night. And Silver, for the third time, lighted a cigarette, scratching two matches, so that both came into a blaze for a moment, though he held them in such a way that none of the light could fall upon his face.

Then a form came across the hotel veranda and rapidly across the street toward him. The starlight showed clearly enough that it was a woman. After her came a long-striding man, a queerly made, light-shouldered fellow who took immense steps.

The girl turned sideways from him and started to run. She thought better of it and turned suddenly to face him.

The two of them were close, by this time, and Silver had slipped back into the thicker shade of an inset doorway, where he was almost invisible.

He heard the girl saying: "You can't follow me. You can't bother me like this, Perry. It's no good! It won't do. I won't have it, Perry. You have no right!"

"Why, I don't know," said the man. "Maybe I have right enough. Maybe I have a sort of duty, Edith, to follow a woman who's run away from her husband the day of the wedding. Maybe I have a duty to show up a fraud. That's what the thing amounts to. Fraud, Edith! You deceived a man. You led him on to marry you, and then you ducked out. Plain fraud, and there are laws that deal with it!"

"You ought to see him," said the girl calmly. "Go see Ned Kenyon, and ask him to open suit against me."

"You're confident in him, are you?" said the other, sneering. "Edith, there's no shame in you, apparently!"

"Shame?" said the girl. "Shame, Perry Nellihan? Doesn't the word blister your tongue a little?"

"Why should it?" asked Nellihan. "I've done only what any man would do to protect my rights! I was robbed of my rights. And you know it!"

"Suppose," said the girl, "that my father had known what you are, instead of merely guessing—what do you think he would have done?"

"The old fool is dead," said Nellihan. "I don't have to think about him. The fact is that he raised me like his own son all my life, and then he cut me off without a penny! Practically."

"More than two hundred thousand dollars—is that only a penny?" she asked.

"Compared with what you're getting!" said Nellihan.

"If I had told father what I knew, he would never have left you even that."

"The point is that you didn't tell him what you knew. That's where you were a fool."

"Very well," said the girl. "Take your hand from my arm, Perry. I don't want you to touch me."

"I'm not good enough to touch you, eh?"

"You're not," said she.

"I've done my share of shady things, perhaps," answered Nellihan. "But I've never done a worse thing than you worked on that poor idiot of a Kenyon."

"I don't think you ever did," she agreed, with a sudden warmth that surprised Silver. "But you know why I had to do it. You know that you worked me into a corner from which I couldn't dodge! There was only that way out for me!"

"I arranged that pretty well," said Nellihan. And he laughed.

Everything about that man was offensive to Silver for more reasons than he could put into words. And the voice, high, thin, nasal, cut into his very brainpan and put his nerves on edge.

"Take your hand off my arm," she repeated.

And the striking muscles in the shoulder of Silver leaped into hardness that refused to relax.

"Where do you want to go?" asked Nellihan.

"That's my affair."

"Girl wandering alone in the middle of the night," Nellihan sneered. "Is your precious thug somewhere around here?"

Silver could see him turn his head suddenly from side to side in eager curiosity.

"If he were," said the girl, "you'd be shaking in your boots."

Nellihan laughed again. "You're wrong, honey," said he. "I'm no saint, but I'm not a coward, either. And when it comes to gun work, I'm not afraid of any man in the West. You ought to know that."

"I only know that you're detestable!" she exclaimed.

"Listen to me, Edith," said he. "You're trying a hard game, and I can spoil it for you. You'll have to talk turkey to me."

"You mean that I'll have to talk money to you?"

"That's what I mean."

"I'd rather give you my blood than a penny of father's money," she answered.

"No matter what you'd rather do," answered Nellihan, "you'll have to talk turkey. I've got you where I want you, and you're a poor fool if you think that I'll let you get out from under before you've ponied up the iron men."

"You haven't a finger's weight of hold on me," she told him.

"No?" said Nellihan. "Don't you suppose that I can put poor Kenyon on your trail? He can make plenty of trouble for you! You'll disgrace yourself and your family—and you won't be able to do a particle of good for the dirty rat you love."

Silver heard her sigh—a long, long breath of disgust and weariness.

"I've told you before," she said, "that you can't do anything with Ned Kenyon. He won't act against me!"

"He will, when I show him how much money he can get out of you. He hasn't enough brains to think in terms of millions, but I can teach him the way of it! I'll put a match to his imagination and set him on fire. Then he'll go after you! Before I did that, I wanted to have a talk with you. That's all. I wanted to show you that you're in my hands!"

"I'm not," said the girl. "For Ned won't act against me. It's hard for a poor, creeping snake like you, Perry, to understand that some men may be honorable!"

"Well," said Nellihan, overlooking the insults blandly, and going straight on, "let me tell you something. I have another hold on you. Do you know that Sheriff

Bert Philips is in this town right now, looking for an escaped crook? Now, then, suppose that I tell him why *you're* up here? Suppose I tell him that, suppose that he gets on your trail—why, what will happen then?"

"You won't do that, Perry," said the girl slowly. "I know that you're bad. But you're not as low as that! You know that my life is smashed to bits. You know that there's no future hope for me. And you won't take away my last chance to find a few minutes of happiness?"

"Won't I?" said Perry Nellihan. He began his snarling, savage, nasal laughter.

"Oh, won't I?" he repeated. "Won't I squeeze you till I've got what I want out of you? Edith, don't be such a fool! You ought to know me better than that. The next thing I know, you'll be on your knees, begging. But words don't matter in my ear, Edith. Hard cash is the only thing that will talk to me!"

"It's true," she said. "And I *am* a fool to talk to you."

"On the other hand," said the man, "take a calm look at the business and see the simple and straight way out. I'm not going to try to take everything. I'm going to make a fair split with you. I'm only going to ask for what I should have by your father's will—one half of the whole estate. Your half will be more money than you can spend. You know that. Why should you grudge me my bit?"

The girl paused, and Silver waited, with tingling nerves, to hear her acquiesce.

Instead, she said in the same quiet way: "You don't quite understand, Perry. I've done one terribly bad thing. I've smashed the life of Ned Kenyon—for a little while, anyway. And that one bad thing is enough. I'm not going to do another. And the worst thing that I can think of would be to turn you loose on the world with money and power in your hands. The very worst thing! Better send a plague into a crowded city than put power in your hands!" She paused an instant. "I've told you what I think. Now get away from me."

"You're going to visit the sheriff with me, my dear," said he grimly. "You're going straight down the street with me till I find the sheriff, and I know where to look for him. Come along!"

He turned her with a violent jerk, so that she made a long, lurching step beside him. Then Silver came like a noiseless ghost behind them.

"Excuse me, señor," said Silver in Spanish.

Nellihan whipped about suddenly, and the force of his turn and the driving weight of Silver's fist combined to strike him down. He bent far backward and then dropped on his side with his arms flung out.

Chapter XIV

BAFFLING PROBLEMS

A MAN who falls like that does not rise suddenly. Silver gave him a single glance, and then said to the girl:

"Quickly, señorita! The two horses at this end of the hitch rack—the gray and the roan! Take the roan. I have shortened the stirrups for you!"

She nodded, saving her breath for her running. And, coming up with the hitch rack, she flashed into the saddle like a man, while Silver jerked loose the knot that tethered the ropes. In a moment he was jogging his horse beside hers down the street.

She had been about to break away at a mad gallop when he cautioned her:

"Señorita, a slow horse is never seen, but a galloping horse is a bonfire. All eyes find it!"

They were turning the corner beyond the next saloon before Silver, looking back, saw the tall form of Nellihan stagger to its feet. They were out of sight around that corner before a sharp, wailing voice began to yammer for help.

The girl bent forward and turned her face to Silver, as though asking permission to gallop the horse. But he made a signal of denial.

That was why they went calmly, unseen, through the town of Kirby Crossing. Only when they reached the upper valley road would Silvertip let the horses gallop. And as the windy darkness blew into his face, he set his teeth hard and tried to understand what he had just seen and overheard.

The whole problem remained vague and obscure in his mind, but he felt that this darkness might be that which goes before the dawn. Nellihan, it was plain, had been raised by the rich father of the girl as a member of the family, though it seemed that he had never been adopted. The man was a rascal, and Alton had suspected it; therefore Nellihan had been cut off with merely enough of an inheritance to support him in comfort. At the same time, Nellihan had managed to use his influence so that the girl's own inheritance was embarrassed. And that embarrassment had forced her, it appeared, to marry Ned Kenyon.

At the thought of Kenyon, the hot anger poured through Silver again, and yet, in spite of himself, he was unable to detest the girl as he had done before. Contrasted with Nellihan, she seemed a saintly figure, almost. And furthermore, what the springs of her actions had been he could not understand, and perhaps when that understanding arrived, he would be able to forgive her, in part, even for the blow she had given to poor Ned Kenyon.

She loved a "thug," as Nellihan had phrased it. Her life, she had said, was wrecked. She was fighting now to salvage from the ruin a few moments of happiness!

As Silver turned these words and ideas in his mind, he was more and more darkly baffled. She was young, beautiful, rich. How could her life be wrecked?

They were almost at the end of the ride when another thought struck like red fire through his brain.

Nellihan! There was a name that began with the letters he was searching for: "Nel—".

And why should it not have been Nellihan? The murderer of Buck must have been tied into this great tangle in some way. The whole thing seemed to possess minute inner relations. He ran over the names—Nellihan, Edith Alton, Ned Kenyon, Lorens, Buck, and finally perhaps some vague connections with the escaped convict, David Holman. These people had entered on the stage from various directions and at various points. When would they be combined in such a way that Silver would be able to understand the entire problem?

But one thing was clear in his mind. Nellihan, he

could swear, was the man who had killed Buck. He had spoken of familiarity with guns. And he was exactly the type of slayer who would shoot from the dark of an open window.

These ideas, rolling across the brain of Silver, were ended by his arrival near the cabin where Lorens lived. He held up his hand as a signal to draw rein, and presently they were dismounting near the cabin of Lorens. He whistled, and Lorens himself came out, hurrying.

"Are you there?" he called.

"Here!" said the girl.

"Thank Heaven for that!" said Lorens.

He told Silver to unsaddle and hobble the horses. He even lingered a moment to look over the animals and he said:

"You got your money's worth, Juan."

Then he turned away beside the girl.

Silver heard her say breathlessly: "Is he here?"

"Not yet," answered Lorens, lowering his voice. "Not yet, but he ought to get here before the morning. Did you bring it?"

"I have it with me—plenty!" she said.

"Good!" said Lorens, very heartily, and they disappeared through the door of the cabin.

Silver went about the unsaddling of the horses, wondering who might be the "he" whom the girl desired to see, and what was the "it" that she had brought plenty of?

He had hardly finished hobbling the horses when Lorens called him.

"Juan," said the man, "can you navigate on very little sleep?"

"Señor," said Silver, "I can lay up sleep the way a cow lays up fat in summer for the winter."

"Can you keep your eyes open all night long?" asked Lorens.

"For three nights, señor, without closing my eyes."

"Good!" said Lorens. "Good man! The lady has told me about the way you handled Nellihan in the town. A very good bit of work, Juan. Come inside and have some coffee, and anything you want to eat."

"No, señor," said Silver. "I have had coffee enough; and I have eaten enough. Now I shall stay outside and watch."

"She wants to thank you, Juan," said Lorens. "Come in for that!"

It was the last thing that Silver wished to go through. He knew the clear, quiet eyes of the girl, and he did not wish to have them fall on him now. What men could not see, she would penetrate with her woman's glance, perhaps. However, there was hardly an easy way of refusing to face her, and he had to follow Lorens back into the cabin.

The girl sat at the wobbly little table in the center of the room, eating cold venison steak with relish. She looked up at Silver, and smiled at him, while he stood with his head inclined, his feet close together, his neck thrust a little forward, and his shoulders bowed a trifle. There is nothing that confuses recollection more than a change of the habitual posture of a man. He could hope that she would never dream of the erect, straight-eyed, rather imperious "Arizona Jim," when she was talking to this awkward Mexican, with the shock of black hair falling down over his eyes.

"It was a very bad time for me, back yonder in the town, Juan," she said. "I want to thank you for helping me. Nobody could have done better. Nobody! For he's a dangerous fellow—that one, Juan. If you hadn't stunned him, he would have been shooting while he fell!"

Silver bobbed his head, made a vague, brief gesture with one hand, and then shrugged his shoulders, as much as to say that what was passed was forgotten, and that the whole affair was not really worth much consideration.

Her manner changed a little. Her head tilted a shade to the side. A certain quizzical look appeared in her face.

Then, rising, she held out her hand.

"Give me your hand, Juan," said she. "Because after we've shaken hands, you'll believe that I won't forget you. And when I find out what you like the most in the world, I'll try to get it for you."

Silver looked down at the palm of his right hand, shrugged his shoulders again, scrubbed his hand against the white cotton trousers he wore, and then glided forward to take the hand of the girl and make a little, ducking bow above it.

When he tried to withdraw his hand, she kept a firm grip on it.

"It was something more than saving my life, that you did for me," she said. "It was giving me a last fighting chance for happiness, Juan!"

"He's tongue-tied," said Lorens, laughing. "Let him go. He's a strong devil, and brave as steel. Juan, you can go outside now, and stand watch. Keep your eyes open. What I expect is one man and one horse. If you find more than one coming this way, give me the alarm. You understand?"

Silver nodded, backed through the door, and was gone.

When he was at a distance, he whistled a bar of a song to register the amount of ground that separated him from the cabin; then he turned and ran for it like a silent shadow, and paused close to the door in time enough to hear her say:

"You're sure about him?"

"Why not?" said Lorens. "He's done enough to prove himself, I'd say! He's worked well for you. He's bought me two fine horses for half the money that I would have had to pay."

"His eyes are light," she answered.

"You find plenty of light-colored eyes in Mexico," said Lorens.

"They must be the exception, though," said the girl.

"Well, perhaps they are."

"So this man Juan is one of the exceptions," said she. "He's an exception in lots of ways. He's bigger than most men. He has heavier shoulders and longer arms. Most peons look stupid, but he has a thinking face. There is a sort of fire of fierceness in him, but when he was standing in front of me, he tried to cover up everything."

"Come, come," said Lorens. "You know how that is—just nervous, just embarrassed in front of the beautiful señorita!" He laughed a little.

"It wasn't embarrassment," she answered. "There wasn't any embarrassment in his make-up. There was no blood warming up his skin. He was cool as a cucumber. And from the look or two I had at his eyes, it seemed to me that he was all set and intent on something, like a tightrope walker a thousand feet off the ground. He was watching his step."

"I don't believe that," said Lorens.

"I hope that I'm wrong," she answered. "But all the while it seemed to me that he was trying to prevent me from having a look at his mind. He hung his head and let his hair fall over his eyes. But it seemed to me that his natural position would be as straight as an arrow, and looking the world in the eye. That's what I felt about him. Perhaps I'm wrong. I know that I'm nervous enough to make mistakes. It's because I'm making my last play to win happiness, and I can't feel secure about anything. Perhaps I have an hour, or a day, or a week—if we're lucky, there may be a month for us. But that's the end! It's for that instant of happiness that I'm fighting and on the alert!"

"All right," said Lorens, his voice growing a little weary and cold. "I suppose I know what you mean. But this fellow Juan—he's all right. If he's not, I'll cut out his heart and take a look at the color of it!"

Chapter XV

THE FUGITIVE

IT is possible to be grateful even to a rogue. Silver was grateful to Lorens. He knew the man was a scoundrel, as dangerous as a snake with poisonous craft, and still he was grateful because Lorens had defended him.

But as Silver drew back into the night again, he kept wondering what might be that happiness for which the girl was willing to do so much.

Now he began to make his rounds of the place, sliding shadowy among the brush and through the trees, rousing up every animal instinct to the keenest pitch of alertness. Nervous hands, as it were, began to reach out from him, and make him aware of everything near by. And yet, for all his caution, for all his spying, when he saw the figure standing at the door of the shack, it was as though the form had risen out of the ground.

He started toward the cabin, swiftly.

For one thing, they had talked about a horseman arriving, and there had not been a hoofbeat even in the distance for a long time. Silver was halfway to the door of the cabin when the shadowy form slipped suddenly through the door into the lighted cabin. Silver had a sight of a man of middle height, of rather a strong build—and as the fellow disappeared from view, the voice of the girl split the very eardrum of Silver with a scream.

He came at the cabin as fast as a tiger runs at easy prey. Through the doorway he leaped with the Colt ready in his hand—and saw Edith Alton Kenyon wrapped in the arms of the stranger, while Lorens conveniently turned his back and had started toward the door.

When Lorens saw the drawn gun, he snapped out a revolver of his own with wonderful speed, but by that time it was apparent that Silver was simply amazed, not attacking. As for the stranger, his face was visible in profile, and it clearly showed the features of the escaped criminal, the pursued murderer, David Holman!

Silver drew back toward the door, entranced. Lorens was beckoning to him to go outside again. And the last he saw was that Holman had made the girl sit down, while he kneeled in front of her and kissed her hands, and looked constantly, hungrily, into her face.

Pale from the prison confinement, his eyes deeply sunk in shadow, it seemed to Silver that David Holman could easily be capable of a murder—but hardly a murder by stealth. It was as strong a face as Silver ever had seen. There was a stonelike quality about the flesh, and there seemed to be a stonelike quality about the stare which he fixed on the girl. He was not speaking. His jaws were hard set. But it seemed to Silver that he had never seen passion so mute or so powerful. That was the index and the key of the man—power, power, and more power!

Looking at him now, it was not at all strange that he had robbed a bank and killed two assistant thieves, but it was just a trifle odd that a sheriff and a posse ever had been able to take him alive, or that he should have told such a cock-and-bull story in his trial.

But there he was in the cabin—that happiness for which the girl had been working and praying; an hour, a day, a week, a month of David Holman had been her dream. And Silver, seeing her in the fulfillment of her wish, found her transfigured. She was crying with happiness; she was a child, and yet she was more profoundly a woman than any Silver had ever before seen in his strange life.

He went out through the door into the black of the night, dazed and confused. He heard Lorens saying, within:

"You two need to talk. I'll take the outer guard, and Juan will keep the door. You can talk right out. He only understands ten words of English."

He came out, calling: "Juan! Come here!"

Silver came slowly back to him.

"You stand here by the door, Juan," said Lorens. "You've made one mistake to-night—that is to say, it might have been a mistake if that had been any man other than Holman. Now, keep your eyes a little wider open. You won't find many as shifty as Holman, but there are others who have eyes, too."

"I shall watch," said Silver grimly. "But if I stay close by the door, I can see only half the night."

"Do as I tell you," said Lorens. "Stand right by the door, and be ready to shoot if anything strange happens. You know what this means, now, Juan. You know that Holman is hunted by the law, with a price on his head. But can you trust us to give you more than the law would give you?"

"Señor," said Silver, "the law has very seldom been my friend. Why should I work for it? And even if I could capture Señor Holman and bring him to the sheriff, ways would be found of cheating a poor Mexican like me. Besides, perhaps the law wants me, also!"

Lorens laughed.

"You're a useful sort of a fellow, Juan," said he. "And you'll be paid your weight in gold, before you're through with this business. There's money to be had out of this affair, and trust me, I know how to get it. This whole business is dripping with coin—dripping! And you shall keep your share. Keep your eyes open. I'm going to walk in a big circle around the house."

He went off into the darkness, whistling under his breath, and Silver pursed his lips in silence.

It was clearly apparent that Lorens was in this for the money, only. He had been the agent, the go-between who had helped the girl to free Holman from prison, in some way. He had distributed the bribes in the proper places, perhaps. And now that the two were together, Lorens intended to watch over them, serve them, and continually squeeze the purse of the girl for his own gain.

In the meantime, it was unpleasant to be an eavesdropper at the door of the cabin, but he could not disobey Lorens. He walked back and forth and tried to shut the voices from his ears, but they kept penetrating his brain constantly.

She was explaining: "Lorens knew one of the trusties very well. He had to pour the man full of money, but at last the thing was done. Some of the bribes were handed out, here and there. And that was why the guards looked the other way when you were escaping. But I don't want to talk about that. The thing's done. You're here. Nothing else matters."

"I want to have everything clear in my mind," said Holman's voice. It was deep, resonant, and yet very quiet. "Where did the money come from? According to your father's will, you were not to have any real income until you married."

Light shot at last through the brain of Silver, as he listened.

The girl said nothing.

"Is that hard for you to answer?" asked Holman.

There was more silence.

"Do I have to tell you?" she asked at last.

"No," said Holman. "I don't want to put a finger's weight of pressure on you. Tell me only what you please."

"Then forget everything in the past!" she urged him. "You know that we haven't long together. They are going to hunt you down. Every minute is one of the last minutes. How can we waste them?"

"Secrets will make shadows between us—that's all," said Holman.

"If I tell you," said the girl, her voice breaking, "you'll despise me!"

A sudden fierce anxiety broke out in his next words: "What thing *have* you done?"

"I found a man who would marry me," she said. "I found—"

"You mean to say that you're married, Edith?" breathed Holman.

"Only in name, only in name!" said the girl. "Listen to me! There was no other way to get the money, and without money I couldn't help you. I found a man— the simplest fellow in the world, only interested in ranching and beef, and such things. I was going to marry him, and then disappear, and leave him a large sum of money, so that he could go ahead and lead the sort of life that he wanted to lead. And when I failed to appear again, he could get his divorce without the slightest trouble because of desertion. Don't you see? Wanted to do him no real harm, but actually to help him, and chiefly, to help you!"

"You *wanted* to do him no harm," muttered Holman. "And then what happened to him?"

She had to pause to rally herself for a moment, apparently, but at last she said: "He grew fond of me. And he—Listen to me! You have to listen. You can't turn away like this. I know it makes you sick at heart. I know that *you* would never have wanted me to do it. But I couldn't dream—"

"Before you married him," said Holman, "didn't you have an idea that he might be getting in pretty deep?"

"I couldn't know for sure. He was such a great, gaunt, simple creature—a caricature of a man. Every one laughed at him—and I wasn't laughing at him. No, no, I was pitying him and liking him. I began to guess that he was fond of me, really. I couldn't tell how much, though."

Holman groaned. Silver heard the spat of a fist driven into the flat of a palm.

"David, what could I do?" cried the girl. "Look at me; tell me what I could do? I didn't dream poor Ned would be of such fine stuff. I thought he might feel one twinge of pain, and then forget all about me in the pleasure of having ten thousand dollars."

Holman's step began to pace the floor.

"What's his name?" asked Holman bluntly.

"Edward Kenyon. He—"

"I've kept my hands clean all my life," said Holman bitterly, "and only for this—to be a condemned criminal escaped from the death house owing to a fraud on the part of a woman. I'm a sponger—a sneaking, cringing cur! I live on a woman; I let her torture other men for me. Ah, that's a picture to remember!"

"If I'd opened my heart and told the whole thing to poor Ned," said the girl, "he would have gone through the form of the wedding. I know that, now, but at the time I was afraid that one whisper of the truth would get out and be the ruin of my plan to set you free, David."

"Hush!" said Holman. "I'm going mad. My brain's turning. I know you've done nothing for your own sake, and everything for mine. It seems that I'm put on the earth to make a fool of myself and a scoundrel of every one else around me. I've put a curse on the people I love. I've made a sneaking, contriving, lying criminal out of you! Out of you!"

Silver heard her begin to sob, not wildly, but a deep, choked sound that told how she was fighting like a man against her weakness. But Holman did not console her.

"About the money," he said. "How much have you spent, so far?"

"I don't know, David. I don't want to think of it. The money doesn't matter. Heaven knows I would have given everything for these moments with you, even if you've begun to detest and despise me!"

"Despise you?" said Holman, in a voice that made Silver stop short in his harried pacing to and fro. "It's myself that's being poisoned by every word that you've told me. I want to know the whole story. How much have you spent?"

"You have to know? You command me, David?"

"I beg you, my dear!"

"It's something over forty thousand dollars."

Silver heard Holman gasp.

"You paid that out to whom?"

"To Lorens, of course. He's handled everything."

"And how much of it is left with Lorens?"

"Nothing, David. He had to spend floods in the prison, through the trusties."

"He used up the entire forty thousand dollars? He didn't put anything in his own pocket?"

"No, David. Not a penny. He has hardly a cent in his wallet, now. He told me only to-day. But I've brought more. I brought another fifty thousand out—"

"Fifty thousand?" cired Holman. "Don't you know that it's enough to get you murdered? Fifty thousand dollars, carrying it around like pebbles in your pocket? But wait a moment. How much does he get of that fifty thousand? How much does he expect?"

"Nothing for himself, David. All that he wants to do is to see you safe. He's had trouble with the law himself, and he took pity on us, David. He himself offered to do what he could. I've never been able to give him a single dollar for his own pocket."

"He sounds like an ideal character," said Holman dryly. "But he doesn't look like one. Not by a mile! Go on, Edith. Tell me how much you'll need to spend now?"

"Just for the moment, a good deal," said the girl. "Lorens is going to arrange everything for us. He knows a section of the mountains where we can be safe, he swears. Perhaps not for days and weeks, but for years. He knows the sheriff of that county, and he knows several others who can be bribed to close their eyes and not know that we're there. It will cost a good deal, to begin with, but then—"

"How much?"

"About forty thousand dollars."

"Forty thousand? Forty thousand dollars, did you say? For a sheriff—and a few others? Who are the others?"

"I didn't ask him. I know that we can trust him. Why are you glaring like that, David?"

"Because the thief is bleeding you! If he spent ten thousand to get me out of the prison, he was a fool. If there's a sheriff to be fixed, either the man can be bought for five thousand, or else he couldn't be touched for five millions. And that's more apt to be the case. Have you given him that forty thousand, yet?"

"Yes," said the girl. "Because he—What are you going to do, David? You're not—"

Holman came to the door of the shack.

"Oh, Lorens!" he called.

"Here!" answered Lorens, and came swiftly. "Anything wrong?" he asked cheerfully.

"I think there is," said Holman. "Come inside. I've been hearing about your money dealings with Edith. I've been hearing about your altruism, too. I've heard that you've just bled her for another forty thousand dollars, you cur! And I'm going to take that money away from you!"

Lorens flashed his hand for a gun.

Holman hit out with a strength that flung Lorens back against the wall and made him drop to one knee. He was half-stunned, but not enough to spoil his shooting at such a close range. And he meant murder. The snarling look in his face was like that of a wild cat about to put his teeth in red meat.

"You fool!" yelled Lorens, above the cry of the girl. "I've trimmed her. And now I'm going to trim you— and collect the blood money on your head!"

"No, señor," said Silver, and he shoved the muzzle of his Colt out of the darkness and into the verge of the light in the room.

Chapter XVI

TO AID AN OUTLAW

THE whole scene was in nice balance. The girl had caught up a Winchester, but dared not swing the muzzle toward Lorens, knowing that she would be too late. So she stood with the rifle in her right hand, her left arm flung out, her face white with fear, and strained in every muscle. Holman, obviously unarmed, was on tiptoe to rush in at the kneeling Lorens, but even Holman, though there was a savage fury in his face, kept himself from moving. And as for Lorens, he was tasting the kill beforehand, with an infinite relish.

But the gleaming of Silver's revolver was enough to change everything. It made Lorens glance to the side.

"You rat!" he yelled. Then he swung into smooth Spanish, saying: "Juan, you know the hand that feeds you. You know—"

"I know, señor," said Silver calmly. "And I know that it is the lady who will spend the money, and not you. Señor, I am sad, but if you don't put down that gun, I shall have to shoot you through the head! Quickly, amigo!"

Lorens turned on Silver a frightful look. Then, in silence, his right hand jerked down inch by inch until the gun lay on the floor. Still his fingers worked on the butt, yearning to snatch it up for action. At last his hand was clear of the Colt.

"Now stand up, señor," said Silver. "Forgive me—but if you make one quick move, my poor thumb on the hammer of this gun will be frightened, and the hammer will fall, and you will go up to join the sky people."

Lorens stood panting, silent. He obeyed Silver's instructions, and turned his face to the wall with both arms stretched high above his head, and in this position, Silver searched him from his hair to the soles of his boots. There was plenty to find, but what mattered most was not the hidden knife and the hidden little two-barrel pistol, but the wallets. One was a good pigskin and rested in the inside coat pocket, but the others were simply a tissue of oiled silk inside the top of each boot.

In the first wallet there was intact exactly the forty thousand dollars which Lorens had been paid on this day. In the two silk swathings, there was almost thirty-two thousand more. Holman counted out that considerable fortune in greenbacks of large denominations.

In the meantime, Lorens was saying to Silver: "What a cursed fool I was! To-night I argued on your side of the fence, too. But I'll tell you, Juan—I'll find a way to come back to you. How you'll pray to die— how you'll beg for hell itself when my hands get to work on you, one day!"

"You hear him, Juan?" said David Holman, in very poor Mexican dialect. "He means poison. You've given me a life that's not worth a rap, but I'm thanking you for it. That's all I can do—thank you. But the lady will try to choke you with a flood of money. Tell us, in the first place, what we can do with this fellow Lorens?"

"Señor," said Silver softly, "what do we do when we find a snake?"

"Kill him? Kill him out of hand?" asked Holman. "You mean that, Juan?"

He stepped back a little, not horrified, but looking at Silver with a sort of pitying curiosity.

"Listen to me, señor," said Silver. "If you try to take him with you, he will escape. If you set him free, no matter what he promises, he'll have the hunters on your trail very soon. I shall not murder him. Let him have back his revolver. We shall both put our guns away, and then it will be fair and even at the start!"

"Good!" said Lorens, with a sudden cry of relief. "I'll do that, Holman! I'll take my free chance with him, first, and with you, afterward!"

Holman shook his head. He lifted a finger at Juan.

"Tie his hands," said Holman. "Then we'll try to think the thing out."

Silver obediently bound the hands of Lorens. He could hardly believe the work that his fingers were doing.

He had found the trail of this adventure when he came out from the upper mountains into view of the plains. He had encountered poor Ned Kenyon and followed him into a maze of strangeness. He had outfronted Buck; he had seen Buck murdered on the verge of speaking the name which began with "Nel—" And he had become the "Mexican" servant of One-eyed Harry Bench, and then of Lorens, only to swing over to the aid of an outlaw with a price on his head!

"I'm wrong to keep him alive, perhaps," explained Holman to Silver, "because I know that he's no great gift to the world. But at the same time, we can't have people killed like that, Juan."

The girl came up close to Lorens.

"Why did you do it?" she pleaded. "I would have given you money. I would have given you anything you asked for. I trusted you. Don't you see, you were only harming yourself? *Why* did you do it?"

Lorens bared his teeth as he looked at her.

"Partly," he said insolently, "because I felt like doing it that way—because I wanted to make a fool out of you—because I intended to suck the blood out of your fortune and leave only a shell of it. And partly I did it because I hated the sight of your face, and the yammering about Holman. Is that enough reason for you?"

He was magnificent as is a fearless beast that is ready to fight to the last, and Silver dimly admired him for the savage that was in him. It was only strange, in the light of this wonderful courage, that the fellow had run away from him that day in the ravine, after firing the first shot. But perhaps that could be explained. There was no money, after all, in the murder of a stray rider, and why should such a man as the great Lorens needlessly leave dead men in his trail, so that the law could find them afterward?

"We'll have to talk things over," said Holman to the girl. "Come outside with me, and we'll make a decision. You, Juan—are you intending to help us?"

"And you shall have as much money—" cried the girl.

"Hush!" said Holman, lifting his hand. "There's something else. He's not doing this all for money."

"No," said Silver. "If they catch me with money, they'll soon know that Juan is a rascal. Let me be a poor man, señor, and when I leave you, give me only what you please. There is no spending of money when a man is buried, señor. And cold tortillas and stale beans are better to eat than lead; neither is it easy to swallow with a rope tight around the neck. Señor, they want you, and they have put a price on you. Señor, they want poor Juan, also. There are people who would pay a price for him, too. So I shall serve you, if you please. I only wish to run back into the town. In half an hour—in an hour, I come again."

"Very well," said Holman. "Trot along."

Lorens began to sneer.

"You see him now. When you see him again, he will have the head hunters along with him! Bah! When was there a greaser who could keep his tongue still?"

Holman merely said: "You can make a noise, Lorens, but you can't make a sound that any one of us wants to hear. Go on, Juan. I'll trust you. I'd rather be dead than give up the hope that there's an honest man somewhere in the world!"

That was what rang in the brain of Silver, as he raced down the valley toward the town again. The hope to find an honest man! It could hardly be mere hypocrisy. And was it true, therefore, that David Holman had been falsely accused, falsely sentenced?

Chapter XVII

AN UNEXPECTED MEETING

IT seemed to Silver that he was in a labyrinth. Now and then he found or thought he found a glimmer of light, but whatever passage he took, led him eventually deeper into profound darkness. But he had the sense of one verity which measured with the simple honesty and gentleness of poor Ned Kenyon—and that was the passion that existed between Holman and the girl.

Silver ran straight on through the town. The dawn was commencing, and the edges of the river were streaked with fire. For this one hour in the day, work on the bridge almost seemed to have ceased. On through the silence of the town, and down the valley he went at full speed.

But when he was still at a distance from the lean-to, he saw the huge bulk of One-eyed Harry in front of the shack, and the smoke of the fire he had kindled rolling slowly off on the wind.

Silver leaned against the shack, panting out words.

"Harry, what's your limit? Are you ready for anything?"

"What are you up to?" asked Harry Bench, the beard puckering all over his face as he pressed his lips hard together.

"Taking an outlaw and his woman where the headhunters won't find him."

Harry Bench grunted. "That's a mean job," he said. "It's been tried, and it don't often work."

"This time it has to work," said Silver.

"What do you get out of it?"

"I get a barrel of fun out of it," said Silver grimly,

"and a chance to put my claws into one or two people who need trouble. *You* get any sort of pay that you want."

"Well," said One-eyed Harry, considering, "I've worked a lot for a dollar and a half a day, and there's been times when I've got two and a half a day, for a short job that was a hard one. But for a layout like this, I'd want double that. They'd have to come across with five dollars a day to me, brother!"

He shook his head to emphasize his demand.

"Ten dollars, call it," suggested Silver, smiling.

"Ten dollars?" said Harry Bench, his eyes gleaming. Then he shook his head again, but this time in denial. "It's too much. There ain't any man that's worth that much for the work he does with his hands. Five dollars a day does for me. No more, and no less. I ain't a hog, Silver!"

"Saddle up, then," said Silver. "Fix my outfit on Parade. Get everything together, and the pack saddle on Parade, and throw some dust on him to tame his color a little. I'm going to sleep a half hour, if it takes you that long."

He lay down on his back, closed his eyes, relaxed his body, his limbs. There was a nervous twitching of his right hand which presently was stilled in turn, and as it ceased, Silver was asleep. Through the noise made by the heavy stride of Bench, through the squeaking of saddle leather, he slept on, until Bench called his name.

Then they went up the valley together, as Bench protested.

"It ain't right to start a long march on an empty stomach, partner!"

"You can live on your fat, for a few days," answered Silver. "We're not apt to have much time for the cooking of fodder, or for the eating of it, either!"

"All right," said One-eyed Harry. "A gent can't expect to travel Pullman when he's collecting five bucks a day. Lead on, son!"

One-eyed Harry put his horse to a trot. Silver rode

the mule with his own saddle on it, and Parade followed on a lead. That was how they got into Kirby Crossing just as the town wakened in earnest and the stores were opened. In the distance they could hear the shouting of voices, and the beating of hammers where the bridge was building.

"Go into the grocery store," said Silver. "We'll need more bacon and general grubstakes for four people. We're going to hit for the tall timber, and we won't be stopping to do any shopping on the way. Pick up what you want, Harry. I'll wait out here and hold the nags."

He sat down on his heels as Harry disappeared, made a cornucopia-shaped cigarette, and smoked with his back against a post of the hitch rack, and his eyes half closed. As a matter of fact, he was half asleep when a voice said:

"Arizona, are you goin' to forget your old friends?"

He turned his head, suddenly, and found Ned Kenyon standing behind him, smiling a twisted smile.

Silver rose quickly to his feet.

"How did you spot me? Who told you that I'd be in this sort of get-up?" asked Silver, scanning the street up and down.

"Nobody told me," said Kenyon. "But there was a kind of look about this here stallion. Four legs like those ain't put under every horse in the world, you know. And every man ain't got a pair of shoulders like yours, Arizona. Not shaking hands?"

"Do you shake hands with every greaser that you meet?" asked Silver.

The twisted smile of Kenyon appeared again. He was so worn about the eyes, his face was so sallow, that he looked as though he had barely dragged himself out of a sick bed.

"All right," said Kenyon. "No offense, Arizona. Shall I go along?"

"Wait a minute," answered Silver. "What brought you up here to Kirby Crossing?"

"There's a man by the name of Nellihan that I'm goin' to meet in a few minutes," said Kenyon. "He got in touch with me. I guess he's not much of a man, partner, but he has an idea about me making some trouble for Edith."

The eyes of Silver narrowed.

"Of course," went on the slow, weary voice of Kenyon, "I don't intend to do that. But I was thinking that through Nellihan, maybe, I'd be able to see her again. I managed to rake up five hundred dollars. I borrowed it here and there, and sold a coupla old saddles. And if Nellihan knows where she is, maybe for five hundred dollars he'd be willing to take me to her."

"Why do you want to see her again, Ned?" asked Silver, setting his teeth hard as pity for his friend mastered him.

Kenyon looked far off across the roofs of the houses. He pushed his hat back and scratched his head.

"Well, it's like this," he said. "If I could kind of tell her that there ain't any hard feeling on my part, and that I'm willing to go and get the divorce, if she wants me to, or keep on being married, if she wants me to, it would sort of ease me, a good bit. And more'n that, to tell you the truth, there's been some minutes—since that day—that I've sort of just wished that I could see her. Just only that. To see her and not say anything, that would be better for me than venison steaks and church music, Jim!"

Silver swallowed hard.

"Nellihan," he said. "Where are you to meet him?"

"Right over there, in that little shack down the street—the one that's got white paint on the front of it and no paint on the rest of it."

"Are you going there now?"

"I'm going there as soon as you're through talking to me."

"Listen to me, Ned. Nellihan is a bad hombre."

"He has to be," answered Kenyon, "or he wouldn't want to make trouble for Edith."

"You don't need to talk to him, if you want to see her. I can take you to her."

"You?"

"Yes," said Silver. He waited for the flush to finish burning the face of Kenyon, and when the pallor had come over it again, as quickly, he said: "But I wonder if it's the right thing for you to do, Ned?"

"Maybe it ain't," agreed Kenyon gently. "I been thinking sort of selfish about it. But maybe it ain't the right thing to do. You'd know better, Jim. If you think that it would hurt her to see me, I wouldn't go."

He waited, tense with anxiety, for the judgment. He was only a child, thought Silver, but never in the world had a more honest child existed.

"If you want to see her, you shall," said Silver suddenly. "I'll take you out there to meet her. But I'd like to lay an eye on Mr. Nellihan, first."

He said it in such a way that Kenyon started.

"What do you mean?" he asked. "You want me to take you over to him?"

"I want you to go over there and start talking to him," said Silver. "Because there's a chance that he knows the look of me, and if he does, he's likely to out with a gun and pepper me. I want you to go in and take his eye, and then I'll try to step inside and have a few words with him. Will you do that?"

"Does it mean guns?" asked Kenyon with a sigh. "I ain't any hero, Arizona. I ain't like you. I got nerves, and bad ones!"

"I don't know what it'll mean," said Silver. "I want to talk to him. You understand? I have something to say to him. That's all. He may start a fight. If he does, I'll have to try to finish it."

Kenyon bit his lip, then nodded.

"I'll go in first, then," said he. "You come when you're ready. So long, Arizona."

He went down the street with his long strides.

A moment later, big One-eyed Harry came out, singing from the bottom of his deep throat.

"Load up the stuff," commanded Silver abruptly. "Get the horses ready. And take them down the street, slowly, mind you. Don't go any farther than that white house, down there. When you get near that, find something to do about the saddle—a girth or something to fool with until you hear from me. Is that clear?"

"Clear as a bell," said Harry Bench. "What new kind of deviltry is up now?"

"It's all a part of one pattern that I don't quite understand, but it's almost clear, now," said Silver. "Do what I say. Be ready to chuck the mule loose, because we may have to start moving faster than a mule gallop."

By this time, the tall form of Kenyon had disappeared through the front door of the white-faced shack, and therefore Silver followed on at once. When he came to the steps that led up to the diminutive veranda, he was glad of the soft-soled sandals he wore. They carried him noiselessly to the door, and as he reached it, he could hear the voices inside.

The penetrating and disagreeable tone of Nellihan was saying: "Business is business, Mr. Kenyon. But to go back to the beginning, you've endured a terrible wrong. That wrong ought to be righted. A fraud has been practiced on you. A terrible fraud. That marriage should not lead to a divorce. It ought to lead to an annulment. As though it never had been. It was a piece of trickery on the part of that girl. And she should be made to suffer for it. Any man with a right sense of his own dignity would be sure to *see* that she suffered for what she's done."

The gentle voice of Kenyon answered, drawling: "I suppose that a lot of people would agree with what you have to say, Mr. Nellihan. But I dunno that I can see it that way. It ain't the money that—"

"Money!" said Nelihan, his voice suddenly lowering. "Money? Do you know what I'm speaking about when I say money? Have you any idea of what you intend to throw out the window?"

"Not any clear idea," answered Kenyon.

"Then listen to me—and I know what I'm talking about. It's my business to know—and I *know!* It's a matter of between eight and ten million dollars!"

Kenyon gasped very audibly; even Silver was shocked by the amount of the fortune.

"I'm putting my cards on the table, Mr. Kenyon," said Nellihan. "I have to say to you that I was made the victim of a crooked will, a piece of fraud engineered by that same girl, and I want you to know that if I can prove that her marriage was an act of fraud, I can have the estate sealed up, make her repay the money she's stolen from the bank, and have two chances out of three to have myself declared the full or the half heir of the whole business. There are my cards, sir. Now what do you think of 'em?"

His hand slapped the table, evidently, at this point.

"Well, partner," said Kenyon, "I dunno what I think. I only know what I feel when you tell me that you're goin' to accuse her of anything and try to prove it by something that I say or do. And I can tell you, man to man, with all the cards face up on the table, that you're an infernal rascal, and that I'll have nothing to do with you!"

"You fool!" gasped Nellihan.

And that was the moment when Silver pushed the door open and stepped inside.

Chapter XVIII

THE ALARM

THE gun of Silver appeared before his body, so the swift hand of Nellihan fluttered, but failed to complete its gesture. He stood in a rather ridiculous, namby-pamby attitude, as though he had been trying to shake mud off his fingers.

"Excuse me, señor, if you please," said Silver.

"Back up into the corner, Kenyon!" breathed Nellihan. "If we've got him between two angles, we'll make him jump! The greaser!"

Kenyon turned quietly to Silver.

"Shall I stay here?" he asked.

"Stand back here near the door," answered Silver, "and wait till I need you."

He kept his speech in Spanish, but Nellihan cried out in the same language:

"Is this a plot between the pair of you? Kenyon, are you a crook, after all? Here—you—what do you want?"

Silver looked at him with a curious penetration. He was seeing Nellihan clearly for the first time, and he thought the man's face was the most detestable he had ever seen. There was something about the entire makeup of Nellihan that was revolting—a sort of cross between the bird and the beast. He had a long, gaunt pair of legs with a pair of great feet on the end of them. He had a hunched back which forced his shoulders forward and kept his head thrust forward at a sharp angle. But no bodily deformity matched his face—a sickly yellow-gray.

The color was not all. The features could be called

handsome, in a way, and a smiling way, at that, but there was a birdlike intensity of brightness about the eyes that turned the blood of Silver cold. The man was something more and something less than human. And if this were the antagonist of Edith Alton, Silver could pity her. It was no wonder that she had been driven to the wall.

"What do you want?" Nellihan was repeating.

"Señor," said Silver, "one might not long ago you killed, in a saloon in Mustang, a man named Buck."

"*You* say I killed him," said Nellihan. "Is there any reason on earth why I should have done it?"

"Yes," said Silver. "The señor hired Buck to murder Señor Kenyon here. And when Buck was about to confess that he was hired, and who had bought him, the señor fired a bullet out of the darkness. He stood safe in the night, and killed this man. But Buck lived to write on the floor!"

"He wrote three letters on the floor, and because they're the first three letters of my name, d'you think that that's a proof against me?" asked Nellihan. "What would the law say to that? He might have been starting to write 'Nelson' or 'Nelly,' or I don't know what!"

"There are not very many names that begin with those letters," said Silver.

"You poor fool," exclaimed Nellihan, "you think that you'll get reward money if you take me back to Mustang and lay the charge against me? Why, the whole town would laugh. There's no motive that could be charged to me!"

"No?" said Silver. "There was first the motive of hiring Buck—to prevent the marriage of the señorita with Señor Kenyon—and then the killing of Buck to close his mouth."

Nellihan leaned over and gripped the edge of the table with both hands.

"That's the case you'll talk up, my Mexican friend, is it?" said he. "You might raise a mob—that's all you could do against me. You never would have a grip on the law. The law would laugh at you. The sheriff would refuse to make the arrest."

A change came over Silver. He stood straighter. The mop of black hair fell back from his eyes, and let the sheen of them strike into the very soul of Nellihan.

"The thing is outside of the law, señor," he said. "But I, also, am outside of the law. I am going to put up my revolver. I know you carry one. If you can murder in the dark, perhaps you can fight in the light. Now, señor!"

Silver flashed his Colt back inside the looseness of his shirt, beneath the pit of the left arm.

But the fear that had been turning Nellihan to stone now was relieved, and the life gradually came back into his eyes. It had seemed to Kenyon, looking on at this strange scene, that the man had been taken into the hand of Silver's greater mind and greater emotion, and crushed. But now he recovered a little, rapidly.

"I see what you are," said Nellihan. "No more a peon than your eyes are black. No more a thug than a saint is. You're one of these romantic fools, are you? Well, I won't make a move to get my gun!"

"If you don't—" began Silver, and suddenly paused.

What could he do? There was nothing he wanted more than to rid the world of this poisonous monster. But he could not shoot down a man who refused to fight.

"I won't," said Nellihan, shaking his head, smiling and sneering. "Some other day—perhaps. Perhaps when I'm myself. But I've had a small shock, and I'm upset. Another day, when I'm myself, I might have the pleasure of putting a bullet through you—whoever you are behind your skin! But not now. I won't lift a hand—and *you* won't do murder!"

Silver stared hard. If ever there had been a temptation toward murder, it was working now in his blood. His breath left him, in the passion of his anger and his digust, and it would have been hard to tell what his next act might have been, when a footfall sounded on the steps of the little house, and the door was flung open by—Lorens!

The gun of Silver flashed toward him, instantly, and seeing the full picture of Kenyon, Nellihan, and Silver gathered together, Lorens slammed the door again and bounded back down the steps, with a yell.

That yell went ringing through the air: "Help! Help! Guns this way!"

Silver rammed the muzzle of his Colt under the chin of Nellihan, and with a swift hand snatched away his two guns.

And he was saying as he "fanned" Nellihan: "There'll be another meeting, Nellihan."

"In which I'll send you to the devil!" said Nellihan.

He was perfectly calm about it. If there was no shame in the man, the lack of it was an added strength for him, it appeared.

"Get your horse!" called Silver to Kenyon. "Get your horse and ride like the devil after me. Keep the spur in its side!"

Then he leaped for the door and out into the street, in time to see Lorens darting into the hotel, still shouting.

The long legs of Kenyon bore him rapidly across the street, diagonally backward. Silver himself reached Parade, and as big Harry Bench mounted his own mustang, throwing the mule adrift, Silver flung himself on top of the pack.

He was working with both hands, as the great horse sprang away, and finally managing to reach down with his hunting knife, he cut the last strap that bound the pack and the saddle to the stallion.

The whole contraption fell crashing into the street, and left Silver on the smooth, rounded, powerful back of Parade.

Looking back, he saw Kenyon streaking a horse after him, with Harry Bench already midway between the two. Still farther back, there was a rout of men tumbling out of the hotel, and mounting their horses.

Silver thundered: "Harry, keep coming, I'm leaving

you, but I'll meet you again in five minutes up the road!"

And he left them—yes, as though they were standing still, for at his call, Parade went away on wings. The green trees blurred together in walls on either side of the road, so great was his speed. It seemed hardly an instant before Silver found himself nearing the shack where Lorens had lived, and as he did so, he saw David Holman ride out on on the gray horse into the trail.

Silver waved his arm frantically, as a signal for haste.

"The girl! The girl! Both of you start on the run!" he yelled.

Holman twisted that cow pony around as though he were an old hand on a cattle ranch, and as Silver checked the stallion opposite the shack, he saw Edith Alton swinging up onto the roan mustang. Then, in one well-formed sweep, the five riders broke away on the trail together.

Silver lingered near the front only long enough to call to Holman to learn how Lorens had escaped, and he was told that the man had been left securely tied, while Holman walked out with the girl for a few minutes. When he returned, just now, he found Lorens gone, and fearing that danger would come, he had saddled both horses and started to ride back a little down the trail to see that all was well.

The story was simple enough. The damage that was done by the fact might be the end of them all, and Silver knew it.

He reined back beside the girl. She gave him a side-long look of agony out of her pinched face. Her look said to him clearly: "You're Arizona Jim! You're the friend of Ned Kenyon, and you've brought him here like a curse on me!"

He answered that look by crying out: "I'm here to help you. So is Kenyon. We're for you, and for Holman. We'll see you through!"

He fell back still farther, and waved cheerfully to

One-eyed Harry Bench, who gave him a tremendous scowl and a shake of the head, as though knowing that his weight would wear out any horse, in a long chase.

Still farther back, along the single file, Silver ranged up beside the white face and the shadowy, sunken eyes of Kenyon. That was what the sight of the girl had done to him.

But Silver shouted at him, almost savagely: "Go up into the lead! You know all of this country like a book. Go up and lay a trail for us that will shake off the men from Kirby Crossing! Go on up to the lead, Ned, if you're half a man!"

Chapter XIX

THE CHASE

THERE were many doubts in the mind of Silver, as he fell back to the place of rear guard on that procession, with the dust raised by the others whipping into his face.

With Parade beneath him, he could sweep away from all danger, easily; and the girl and Holman were well mounted, also. But the weight of Harry Bench was a ponderous load for a horse to bear, and Kenyon was a clumsy rider, and his mustang not very fast of foot. The speed of the party would have to be the speed of the slowest member in it, unless he could devise a way to split the group into sections.

What the men from Kirby Crossing wanted, of course, was David Holman, and the price that was on his head. If Bench and Kenyon, being the worst mounted of the group, could be shunted aside, it was not likely that any of the men of Kirby Crossing would tail after them. But now they left the trees and entered a great ravine where there was not even a bush or a rock to make a hiding place, and no canyons opened on either side. Perhaps a glacier, in the dead ages, had plowed out this enormous trench. At any rate, it seemed to Silver that Kenyon was leading the party into a hopeless trap, for the pursuers were rushing out from the trees in turn, and racing up the gorge.

He looked back, and gauged them. There were a full score of head hunters who had answered the call of Lorens and joined in the chase. Except for Lorens himself, five thousand dollars, even if divided into twenty parts, would give a handsome sum to each of those fellows. And if Lorens despised a cash reward as small as this, he would be gratified by revenge.

They made a formidable couple, hunting together—Lorens and Nellihan. And behind them, no doubt, was a hardy assortment of fighting men. Silver, scanning them, thought that every one of the lot rode like a veteran horseman.

He ranged Parade forward to the side of Kenyon, who galloped in the lead.

"They're gaining on us, Ned!" he said. "Some of 'em are eating up the ground. We've got to get into cover or broken ground before long, or they'll scoop us up."

Kenyon pointed ahead.

"You can't see it yet," he said, "but half a mile ahead there's a ravine opening on the right. It twists back into the mountains, and it's filled with cover. Three men could hold off three hundred Injuns in that ravine."

Silver pulled back to the rear again. David Holman joined him.

"Go back beside the girl!" Silver commanded him. "I don't need you."

"You've turned from Mexican into white, Juan, have you?" said Holman. "She tells me that she's recognized you at last—that you're Arizona Jim—that you're the friend of—of her husband!"

His face twisted as he said that.

"Whatever I am, and whatever Kenyon is," said Silver, "we're in here to help you. You get back beside the girl."

"While you stay back and catch the bullets that fly?" asked Holman.

He smiled a little, then eased the Winchester that slanted in a saddle holster under his right leg.

"I'll stay back here with you," said Holman calmly.

Silver protested no longer. Those men from the town of Kirby Crossing were gaining too rapidly, and the mustang that carried the bulk of One-eyed Harry was beginning to labor and grow unsteady of foot. Loud yells came from the pursuit. Each man rode as if for prize. And the cold sweat beaded the forehead of Silver as he heard the whoopings.

But there, on the right, opened the mouth of a narrow canyon. It looked not so much water-worn, as simply a crack in the rocks. Kenyon led the way into it, and from behind, Silver heard a redoubled shouting that seemed to be of triumph. He looked back. He saw waving hats and hands, and one of the punchers shooting a stream of bullets into the air.

That was the way men acted when they rejoiced, but why should they be triumphant now?

For the entrance to the ravine seemed to Silver to promise them an ideal retreat. The little canyon wound crookedly back into the highlands, and the floor was covered with shrubs and with rocks that had fallen from the walls. But as they turned the first elbow bend, a shout of woe went up from Kenyon.

Silver saw the trouble at a glance, and an explanation of the exultation of the men of Kirby Crossing. For the lofty wall on one side of the valley had been shaken loose by an earthquake, perhaps, and now the gorge was choked almost to the top with a mighty confusion of broken rock, great stones that had broken square or jagged, and were heaped in ten-ton fragments.

"Climb! Climb! Climb!" yelled Silver.

He took the lead to show them how to do it. There would be no time to dismount and gradually maneuver the horses up the face of that dangerous pile. The men of Kirby Crossing would be at them in no time, and Silver flew Parade right at the mighty barrier.

Right and left, like a mountain goat, Parade sprang up three- and four-foot stages. His feet were slipping; his iron shoes were striking fire at every move, but yet he went on swiftly. Nothing but his seventeen hands could stretch from one footing to the next, perhaps. But up to the top he went, dislodging a great boulder near the crest of the barrier.

Silver, dismounting, shouted the order that would make the stallion lie flat on his side, safe from rifle fire. Silver himself turned, rifle in hand, and dropped to his knees, for his first purpose in riding up the wall had been to get into a position from which he could cover the climbing of the rest.

He saw the boulder that had been dislodged leap down an irregular step or two, then bound outward. It missed the head of Kenyon by a hair's breadth, and smashed to bits on the rocky floor of the ravine. Kenyon himself was struggling up among the rocks. He had given up trying to lead his horse, which had promptly balked. In fact, only one horse of the outfit was climbing, and that was the gray which Holman had been riding. The tough mustang seemed to be cat-footed as it followed, though far less swiftly, where Parade had showed the way with a rider on his back. Big Harry Bench was leading in the climb, close behind the mustang, and David Holman was a little below him, helping the girl.

That was the picture at the feet of Silver when the leaders of the posse came sweeping around the corner of the canyon wall. He hoped, in his heart, that Lorens and Nellihan would be among the first, for he wanted with all his heart to put lead into them. But they were not among the leaders, and Silver could not shoot point-blank at strange men, whose hands might be clean.

He could fan their faces with his bullets, however.

Lying flat, with his rifle on a rest, he pumped six shots in rapid succession among the riders, and every bullet made some one of them jump or duck as though it had actually whipped through his flesh.

They whirled their horses, yelling, swinging forward like Indians along the necks of their horses, to make themselves into smaller targets. In a moment they were out of view, at the same time that the gray mustang gained the crest of the rock pile. Silver caught the horse, threw the reins, and let it stand. Then he lay down once more to guard the climbing of his party.

Presently, guns began to clang. The men from Kirby Crossing had dismounted, and lying behind rocks, or standing behind the edge of the elbow turn in the canyon wall, they opened fire. Two or three bullets sang in the air over Silver. Others thudded against the boulders farther down.

He answered that fire. He had only an occasional glance at the sheen of steel gun barrels, but a howl of pain answered his third shot.

An instant later, it was echoed by a cry of agony from Edith Alton. Silver looked down, in horror. It was not the girl that had been struck, however, but David Holman, who lay helpless, wedged between two rocks.

Kenyon saw that from beneath, and struggled up to help the wounded man. Greater help came from above, however, for huge One-eyed Harry sprang down, caught up Holman's body as though it were a sack of bran, and bore it unaided over the top of the rocks.

There was only one reason why every one of the climbers was not shot down, and that was the rapid fire which Silver opened on every glint of steel. Not a single rifle was answering him when Kenyon helped the girl up the last step, and the whole party ran stumbling forward into safety.

Silver looked back. He could see a red stain spreading over the back of Holman's coat, as Bench carried him trussed across his shoulders. The bullet seemed to have gone right through the center of Holman's body! He marked the place where it had entered; he marked the white agony in the face of the girl as she ran to her over. Then he shouted his orders.

They were to strip Holman to the waist and examine the wound, and dress it as well as they could. While the girl and Kenyon did that, Bench would clamber onto the high ground on the adjoining side of the rock heap, and cut down two straight, light-bodied saplings for the making of a litter. He, Silver, would try to keep the enemy back while these preparations were made for carrying Holman with them in their retreat.

No one answered him by word of mouth. Each dumbly set about the execution of his appointed task while Silver turned back with a freshly loaded rifle and gave his attention to the ravine below.

The men of Kirby Crossing were not apt to try to charge forward from their angle of concealment. They were more likely to try to climb the wall of the gorge at their left, and so come out on a level with their quarry. They would not be in very great haste however. For they knew that Holman had been shot, and they would not be likely to imagine that the other three men would attempt to take the desperately wounded man along with them in the retreat. No, Holman was their prize, and Hollman they would soon have!

Silver could not help agreeing with that thought. Hope had dwindled in him to a vanishing point, as he glanced back from his scanning of the valley and watched the girl and Kenyon at work. It was a strange sight to see the three together, the girl and the man she had wronged working with a single devotion to save her lover.

They had stripped Holman to the waist. He was still senseless. And now they were bandaging him with strips torn from shirts and the underskirt of the girl. Kenyon was lifting the body, and the girl was passing the long strips around it. She had made a pad over the wound where the bullet entered that body, and another over the more gaping mouth whereby it had torn its way out.

Were they bandaging a man already dead, or breathing his last?

Silver looked back toward the ravine again, when he heard the voice of Holman say distinctly:

"The rest of you go on. Arizona—and the rest of you. You'll get long terms if you're caught helping an outlawed man to escape. And I'm not worth it. The life's running out of me. In another hour it won't matter whether you've stood by me to the finish or not! Arizona, take charge—make the rest of 'em march on!"

Chapter XX

THE ROPE BRIDGE

SOMETIMES to a lucky father there comes a moment when his son reveals by some word or some act the promise of a mind and a soul worthy of taking its place among the good and the strong men of the world. And in that moment all the pain of labor that has been spent, the anxiety, the fear, the groaning time of disappointment, are repaid, and a calm happiness comes over him.

So it was with Silver when he heard Holman speak. Much had been ventured for this fellow. Not only Silver's safety, but Bench and poor Ned Kenyon were endangered exactly as the wounded man had pointed out. But that danger mattered nothing now, because the words of Holman proved that he was worth all that could be done for him.

He heard Kenyon saying: "There ain't any use talking. Arizona won't leave you. And I won't leave you. And I reckon that Harry Bench won't chuck you over, neither. Here he comes now!"

Bench had duly brought back the stripped sapling poles that Silver demanded. The ends of them were tied to the saddle of Parade and of the gray horse. Across the center of them a blanket was lashed to complete the litter, and Silver helped lift the wounded man into it.

He made one final protest.

"Waste is a bad thing, Arizona,'" said he. "Why do you waste yourself and all the rest, Arizona? The life is running out of me. It's no good fighting when the fight's lost beforehand!"

He even turned to the girl, saying: "Tell them, Edith. Tell them that they've done enough already. If they try to go on with me, they'll simply be scooped in by Lorens and the rest. I'm what those fellows are after. They'll leave the trail if they get me!"

The girl said nothing. She kept her green eyes fixed upon the face of Holman and suffered silently.

"If you've got breath enough to chatter like this, you've got breath enough to live for a while," said Silver. "Harry, you can't lead Parade. He'd try to eat you. I'll have to take him along. Ned will see the gray doesn't pull back. Edith, you walk beside Holman. Harry, you're the rear guard. Watch yourself, because those fellows are going to be after us on horses before long!"

It was the logical danger. After the men of Kirby Crossing gained the high ground to which Silver's party was now passing, the pursuers would be sure to get at least some of their horses over the rocky barrier, and so be able to rush the fugitives.

There was one good feature. The whole of the upland was covered with boulders, with big brush, and with copses of pine; and if they could make a few trail problems, they might keep away from the pursuit until darkness gave them a real chance to slip away.

Behind them they heard not a sound as they began to climb the side of a mountain, and when they were well up, Silver looked back and halted Parade for an instant. They were among big pine trees, but through the trunks they had distant glimpses of the scene below, where the entire posse was at work bringing up unwilling horses to the top of the barrier. Already eleven horses were up. Two more came to the top, and instantly these were mounted, and the diminished posse rushed off in pursuit.

"Ned," called Silver, "they'll be on our heels in twenty minutes. Is there any way out for us?"

"There's no way except one that a horse can't walk!" said Kenyon. "There's nothing but the old rope bridge across Whistling Canyon. If the ropes ain't rotted away!"

No way except one that a horse could not take? It meant leaving the gray behind, then; above all, it meant that Parade would be lost. Silver, jerking his head suddenly back, looked up at the sky and groaned.

"You've done a grand piece of work and you've made a good try," called the voice of David Holman. "But it's no use. Put me down here, Arizona. Heaven bless you for what you've done, but drop me here and go on to clear your own heels before the fire gets at them!"

Silver answered harshly: "Save your breath, Holman. You may be needing it before night! Ned, which way to the bridge?"

Kenyon called the directions. Silver led the way, and they went slowly around the side of the mountain—slower, it seemed, than the crawling of a snail—while behind them horses were galloping on their trail! But now they came out on the side of Whistling Canyon and saw the bridge. It was a thing to take the breath, a fifty-foot stretch of ropes sagging across a gulch a hundred yards deep. And those ropes not only looked small, but they were whitened by long weathering.

The floor of the bridge was a mere cross-lashing of small ropes, stiffened by sapling poles to give a steadier footing. There was a guide rope stretched three feet above the frail bridge, and the whole supple structure was swaying in the wind that had given the canyon its name.

Silver set his teeth and looked across the span. Then he stepped on the edge of the bridge and strained on the ropes with all his might. They gave very little as he pulled up the slack. But though their strength might sustain his single weight, how would it support two men in the center, with the burden of Holman borne between them?

He dared not risk that. Two at a time would be the greatest weight that he dared to put on the ropes, he felt.

Quickly the litter was unfastened from the stirrups, and, lifting Holman to a sitting posture, Silver said to him: "Hang your arms over my shoulders. I'm going to carry you."

"No!" cried the girl. "You can't balance yourself with Dave on your back. You'll both——"

Silver raised his hand.

Holman said gravely: "You know what you're doing. I'm only a fool if I try to stop you. But Heaven help you, Arizona, when you get out there in the center, if the wind starts the bridge pitching!"

Silver grunted. The fear of the thing was already a cold stone in his stomach.

"Go first, Ned," he commanded Kenyon. "Sneak across and try it out for us. If it holds one man, we'll chance it with two."

Kenyon, yellow-green with terror, cast one glance at the girl, winced back a step, and then marched straight out onto the ropes! Silver watched him, amazed at the nerve power that the poor fellow had managed to rouse in the time of need. Right out across the bridge went Kenyon, with stealthy, short steps, one hand gripping the guide rope. He reached the center. His weight there, fighting against the pressure of the wind, made the whole bridge shudder violently. But still he went on, perhaps for no other reason than because to pass on was easier than to turn back!

And now he had leaped the last yard or so and lay face down, safe on the farther side.

Big Harry Bench came grunting up, exclaiming: "They're milling around down there on the side of the mountain, but they'll find the trail again in a minute. What the devil is this here? I been told I was goin' to die by the rope, but I never seen *this* kind of a picture of my finish! Here, Silver! I'll pack him over! I can do it more easy than you!"

"Pack yourself over—and shut up," said Silver, and rose with the feeble arms of Holman hanging over his neck. He gripped those arms with one hand. The other he placed on the guide rope, and the last he saw before he stepped onto the peril of the bridge was the girl on her knees, her face buried in her hands, unable to look on.

No, there was one thing more he saw, and that was the beautiful head of Parade thrusting close to his face with pricking ears, and eyes filled with mild inquiry. He tried to speak, but no words came to Silver. It was the end of the horse for him, no doubt. Those men of Kirby Crossing would pick up the great horse as their rightful prize. And they would soon learn that it was a prize worth more than the blood money they could collect on poor David Holman.

He stepped straight past Parade and started out onto the bridge.

Step by step he went on, his teeth hard-set. And at his ear he heard the gasping breath of Holman, for, of course, the man was enduring the most frightful agony.

Silver tried to keep his glance only on the floor of the bridge, but that floor was hardly two and a half feet wide, and again and again his eyes slipped over the side and reached the bottom of the ravine, where the waters of Whistling Creek were churning themselves white and sending up an ' ominous voice into the shrillness of the wind. He saw a blasted pine, a naked trunk at the edge of the water, and it looked hardly larger than a walking stick.

One false step—

And he could not trust to the guide rope except for the most treacherous bit of aid in steadying himself. He had to keep his balance almost entirely by his feet alone. It was hard enough at the side; it was a desperate business in the center, for the wind came in gusts and struck the ropes hammer blows.

But the center had been passed, and now his courage and his hope revived together. He was moving forward more rapidly when suddenly the body he carried slumped down, the full weight jerking on his shoulders as the knees that had gripped his hips lost their hold.

He staggered. For one instant he swayed far to the right. The hands which clutched the arms of Holman shuddered and almost relaxed their grip. It seemed that they were already falling, the two of them together—and then the wind knocked at the bridge and seemed to put it again under the feet of Silver.

He walked on. The feet of the senseless man he carried were dragging behind him. But there was Ned Kenyon waiting for him, holding out both hands, shouting with a white, distorted mouth, words of encouragement. So he made the last steps and stretched his burden safely on the ground.

A dead man? No, the lips of Holman were moving, though they made no sound. Neither had there been a fresh hemorrhage. And Silver began to breathe out loud groans of relief.

"Look at her!" he heard Kenyon saying. "There's no fear in her except for him. There's no care in her except about him, Jim! Look!"

She was already halfway across the bridge, moving more rapidly than any one who had passed before her. She seemed almost to run up the last big of the way, and now she was dropping to her knees beside Holman.

Silver merely said: "He's living, and he's going to keep on living. I've forgotten the litter. No, there's Harry Bench bringing it. Ned, there's a man with a heart as big as his body!"

For Harry Bench, with the long poles of the litter balanced on his shoulder, was now coming steadily, smoothly across the bridge, and in a moment he was with them.

"Get him on the litter," commanded Silver. "Quick, Harry—take his shoulders—there we have him. Ned, cut the ropes at this end, and we'll leave a jump that the Kirby boys can't take!"

"Send him back!" shouted Kenyon. "Look, Jim! He's trying to cross the bridge to join you!"

Silver, whirling about, saw that the great stallion had actually started out on the bridge, and was already a little distance from the farther side. Crouching low, his head thrust far out and down, the golden horse was stealing like a cat across the bridge. And he could not be sent back; he was already committed to the crossing.

Chapter XXI

HOLMAN'S STORY

A STUPOR came over Silver as he watched. Love drew the great horse to him, he knew. But that crossing could not be made. Even if the ropes could endure the strain of that great body, Parade could not keep his balance against the battering strokes of the wind, whose force was increasing now. He had no hand to place on the guide rope and help him across the worst moments of the way.

He would fall, and the creek beneath would grind his glorious body to shreds. There would be one crimson flowing of the water, and there the end of Parade! And Silver thought of the other days when he had made the great march behind the starving wild horse, and how they had journeyed up the burning valley, and drunk together from the same spring!

He had not conquered Parade. It had been simply that in the end they had given their trust to one another. And because of that trust, Parade was crossing the bridge, trembling, crouching with terror, feeling his way like a cat, but always with his ears pricked.

Silver heard the voice of Holman saying: "His horse, Edith—he's giving his horse for me, too—and he'd rather give up half his life than that!"

Then the girl was suddenly at Silver's side, holding his arm with both hands, looking not at Parade, but at the master of the horse. She was saying:

"He's going to win across. God won't let him fall! God won't let him fall!"

Silver heard her words out of a dream. She believed them, perhaps.

Parade was coming to the center of the bridge, while the ropes groaned loudly under his great weight, and the wind screeched like an angry fiend as it smote that frail structure. With every gust the huge body of Parade shuddered, and the whole bridge swayed.

If there were some way to hearten him; if there were something that could be done!

For Parade had stopped in the very center of the bridge, at last totally overcome by fear. The slight twist of his head to the side made Silver know that the horse had given up hope and was thinking of the way back. Thinking of that—and staggering and swaying, his balance going. And every hair of his golden hide was drenched now with the nervous sweat.

And Silver?

He broke suddenly forth with a hoarse singing, an old song that has comforted many a night herd when it was bedded down on the trail, a song that Silver had sung more than once when he and Parade were marching through the cold and the wind of some winter evening:

> "Oh, I'm riding down the river,
>   With my banjo on my knee;
> I'm riding down the river,
>   And no one else with me.
> Strike up that banjo, strike her!
>   A song has gotta be.
> Strike up that banjo, strike her!
>   That banjo talks to me."

As Silver worked into the song, his voice gained a ringing power and struck boldly across the canyon through the wind.

What meaning had it for Parade? Perhaps it meant for him as much as the touch of his master's hand on the reins, sending sure, calm messages from the brain of the man to the brain of the horse. For suddenly the stallion was no longer swaying, crouched till his belly almost touched the ropes. He was standing higher; he was moving forward with cautious steps; he was nearing the place where Silver stood with the agony in his eyes and the song on his lips. Now the outstretched hand of the master touched the head of Parade, and now the great horse stood shivering on safe ground!

The girl threw her arms around the wet neck of the stallion, but Silver merely laid his hand on the broad forehead of the horse and spoke words that had no meaning.

A moment later the knife of Kenyon had slashed the ropes, and the length of the bridge swished into the air and hung dangling from its moorings on the farther edge of the canyon.

After that Silver took up one end of the litter, and Harry Bench the other.

No one spoke. Something like fear was in their faces as they pressed forward among the rocks and the shrubbery, for they felt that they had been privileged to witness a miracle.

Hardly had the shrubbery closed behind them when they heard the beating of the hoofs of horses and the yells of angry men. The pursuit had reached the end of its tether for that day, at least!

They went on by slow stages to the end of the day, and so worked through the rough of the mountains to the projecting shoulder of a peak from which they could see the foothills sloping down in diminishing waves to the plains beneath. In the sunset time they could see the faint golden sheen of the Tuckaway River, that wound through the level, and the windows of the town of Tuckaway itself glimmer like distant fire for a few moments before the sun went down.

It was necessary to rest at this point, for though the wounded man endured the pain of travel without a word, he would have to have sleep. It was certain, now, that the bullet had avoided injuring any vital organ; neither had there been any great loss of blood. He was simply weak from shock, and time would be needed for the healing of the wound.

It was the plan of Ned Kenyon, who knew the whole

district perfectly, to leave the mountains before sunrise and trek out into the plains—chiefly because the pursuit would hardly expect such a move, and moreover because he knew of certain obscure shacks here and there where they could lie up with little danger of being discovered. As Kenyon put it: "We'll sit down right in front of their door, and they'll burn up their horseflesh combing the mountains for us."

The choice of that particular mountain shoulder was largely dictated by a lucky chance, for as they reached the ledge and put down the litter to take breath, a mountain sheep was seen far, far above them, looking out at the sunset. Silver's rifle clipped that prize through the head, and the sheep came pitching and rolling the great distance down to the flat, where the party waited.

Food was needed, and this was a prize. Kenyon and One-eyed Harry cut up the sheep rapidly while Silver arranged half a dozen small fires, which he fed with the wood of dead and dry brush. The changing half lights of this time of day would make it very difficult for an eye even close at hand to distinguish the misting breaths of smoke that rose from those small flames, each a mere handful of brightness. And presently there was mutton roasting on wooden spits at each of the fires.

They had not even salt; they had cold spring water instead of coffee; but ravenous hunger after the day of labor made them eat like wolves. And they were sheltered from observation for this one night, at least. Somewhere, perhaps not a mile away, the men of Kirby Crossing were bivouacking. Or had they turned back and given up the hunt? That was hardly likely—not with Nellihan and Lorens among their number to urge them on. But for this night it was almost impossible that they could close in on their quarry any farther. To-morrow the peril would recommence. This was an interlude of peace to be enjoyed to the full.

Holman was the amazing man to Silver. With every hour he seemed to be gaining in strength. He ate a share of the roasted meat, and afterward he smoked a cigarette which Silver made for him. He had been bedded down on a soft pile of pine boughs, and after his wound was washed and fresh pads placed over the bleeding places, and the bandages again drawn into place, he seemed to be suffering no great pain. The girl sat beside him silently. There seemed to be no sky, no earth, no day and no night for them; they looked only at one another.

Holman tried to express thanks to Silver. He was cut off abruptly.

"If you've got any breath to waste," said Silver, "use it to tell me that the yarn I've heard about you is a lie. You didn't plan the robbing of the bank with 'em. What you told in the courtroom *was* the truth?"

Silver had discarded his black wig. He had scrubbed away the dark stain on his skin. And now, through the glimmer of twilight, the girl and Holman could see the points of gray in his hair, like an incipient horn growing up above either temple. That suggestion gave him a touch of wildness, and his ragged clothes intensified the strangeness—that and the way the stallion always grazed near by, sometimes coming over to sniff at the master, sometimes lifting a lordly head to study every scent that blew toward them on the wind. It was patent that this man was at home in the wilderness, and that he asked for no better companionship than that of the stallion alone. He seemed to Holman, particularly, like a wild, migratory animal which for a moment was crouched among them, and would presently be gone, no man could tell whither.

"What I told in the courtroom," said Holman, "sounded like cock-and-bull, but it was the truth. Truth has a silly face a good many times."

"Who was behind that pair of thugs, if you were not?" asked Silver.

"George Wayland. Buster Wayland."

"Who's he?"

"He used to be vice president of the bank. Simonson was the president, and Wayland the vice president.

Now Simonson is out, and Wayland is the whole thing. He's the big boss."

"You hadn't robbed the bank of a hundred thousand or so before the safe was opened that night?"

"How could I have been such a fool?" asked Holman. "I have money enough of my own. I was working in that bank to get experience. That was all. I wasn't gambling. I wasn't buying stocks on a margin. As a matter of fact, my salary was small, but I lived inside of it."

"Who *did* rob the bank, then?" asked Silver.

"Wayland."

"Are you sure?"

"Yes. I saw him do it."

"When?"

"On the night when they put guns at my head and made me go down to the the bank. There were not just the two of them. Wayland was along."

"If he wanted to rob the bank, why didn't he do it without you?" asked Silver.

"Simonson and I were the only ones who knew the combination that unlocked the safe."

"And they picked on you instead of Simonson?"

"Simonson wouldn't be apt to rob his own bank. It was in good shape. And besides, Simonson would have fought back. They picked on me because they knew that I was yellow."

"That doesn't wash," said Silver. "You're not yellow."

"Perhaps not now. But I was then. And Wayland knew it. He'd bullied me in small things, and I had lain down. As a matter of fact, when they put guns to my head, I was so scared that I could hardly move. They had to carry me out of the house I was in—or almost carry me. When we got to the bank, my hands were shaking so that I could hardly work the combination. But I opened the door of the safe for 'em—and because of that, I deserved everything that happened to me afterward. Oh, I doubtless deserved even more."

"No!" whispered the girl.

Holman went on calmly: "Wayland had a small interest in the bank, even though he was vice president. He wasn't much of a banker. And he saw his chance to make a stake for himself. Right there in the bank, they split the loot into three parts. Wayland took one part. The two yeggs took two parts. It was an equal division, except that Wayland took most of the hard cash and gave the others more of the securities. Then the yeggs went on with me. You can see how the scheme would work out. The bank robbed, the door of the safe opened, and with me gone from town, the whole suspicion would point at me. When I was taken, I might shout my head off accusing Wayland, but he would simply laugh at me. He could depend on the crooks to keep me away for a day or two, he thought.

"Well, matters went a little differently, but all the better for Wayland. The sheriff, happening by in the middle of the night, after Wayland had said good-by to the thugs and they'd started off with me, made things hard for them. Wayland got back home to his bed, but as he was turning in, the thugs were being run out of the town, and I was carried along by them. They were sticking to the promise they'd made to Wayland to the last. The posse came after us. Finally we got clear, and I saw that I was ruined unless I managed to do something.

"I got desperate enough to forget some of my fear. The two yeggs despised me. They had reason to despise me, you see. And so I had a chance to get a gun from one of them. I knew a bit about shooting. And I had them by surprise. I nailed them both, and then tried to get away with the loot they'd taken. My idea was that if I could get back to Tuckaway with the money, it would be proof that I'd been innocent. But when the sheriff and the posse hove in sight, I lost my head and tried to bolt again. I played the fool. They caught me. The money was on me, and when I tried to tell my story, I was laughed at.

"Now see how the thing worked out for Buster Wayland. As soon as I was brought in, he swore that if I

had robbed the bank that night, I had been probably
robbing it before, and covering up the thefts in my
books. They made an accounting and found the bank
terribly short. Of course, that was because Wayland
still had his share of the loot! When the bank was
found short, a run on it started. Simonson had no
ready cash. When the funds in the safe were used up,
Wayland was in a position to hold a gun to Simonson's
head.

"Simonson had to sell out his shares in the bank for
next to nothing. And Wayland simply stepped in and
filled the breach with part of the stolen money. It gave
him the name of a hero and a public benefactor, too.
He wound up owning the bank; he'd established himself
as an honest man and a strong one. The big ranchers
and mine owners in the district, I understand, have
been hauling their accounts out of other banks and de-
positing with the Wayland Bank in Tuckaway—because Wayland can now pose as the financial giant, the
public-minded citizen, the man to whom honesty meant
more than hard cash, the fellow who flung his private
fortune into the breach and saved the widows and or-
phans. Simonson died of a broken heart. I was sentenced to die. And Wayland can loll back in his
easy-chair and smoke some more of his fat cigars."

He ended without raising his voice. He had spoken
rather as one who reads a story aloud than as one who
tells it. It was almost pitch-dark, and out of the darkness came the voice of Silver, saying:

"I have to be taking a trip to Tuckaway tonight!"

Everyone protested, except One-eyed Harry. He
said: "I ain't big enough to try to change his mind.
Then how can the rest of you think that you got a
chance?"

Holman said: "But I know the difficulties more than
the rest of you. Arizona, let me tell you that Wayland
keeps guards about him night and day. He knows how
to win the faithful services of crooks, perhaps because
he's such a crook himself. If it were Wayland him-

self—well, you might do something, though I don't see what!"

"I won't know till I'm on the spot," said Silver. "But I'm going to Tuckaway. Tell me one thing more. When the posse reached the second of the yeggs you had shot up, he was alive; and as he died, he confirmed the yarn that Wayland was to tell later. Why didn't he tell the truth as he died?"

"Because he wanted to be sure that he'd knotted the rope around my neck before he cashed in his chips. I'd killed him; he wanted to be the death of me; and he'd already gone over the story with Wayland in case of need."

"That's all logical," said Silver.

He went aside with One-eyed Harry and Kenyon, and said to them: "It's about an hour's ride from here to Tuckaway. That means two hours for going and coming back. Besides, I don't know how long I'll be in the place. It may be near to sunup before I arrive here again. Be on the watch. Lorens and Nellihan have brains in their heads, and they know how to use 'em. They're fighting men, too. And anything that a snake could do, *they'll* do. One of you had better keep on watch half the night, and one the other half. Ned, come and step away with me."

He led Kenyon aside and found his hand in the darkness.

"You're going through hell," said Silver, "but you're going through it like a man. I know you'll put up a fight if the pinch comes."

"I dunno," said Kenyon. "I ain't much of a fighting man, but I hope I'll do my best. And it ain't exactly hell that I'm goin' through, Arizona. The fact is, it's like bein' in the middle of a sort of a sad dream, but not wanting to wake up from it."

Silver wrung his hand and went to the girl. She moved slowly beside him through the darkness.

"Oh, have hope," said Silver. "There's luck with us, or we couldn't have lasted this long."

"We've had you from first to last," she answered.

"You've saved us before, and I can't *help* hoping, so long as you're in the fight!"

"Perhaps the whole thing is for the best," he said. "Tell me one thing—were you very fond of Holman before he got into this trouble?"

"I was always fond of him," she answered. "But he seemed a little weak and soft. He wasn't what he's grown to be. But when I heard what he was accused of, only one thing crashed into my mind—that he'd fought two criminals and beaten them with their own weapons."

"I almost knew it," said Silver. "He never would have discovered himself if the big pinch had not come. And you would never have discovered him, either. There's Nellihan, though? What about him? Is he as much of a snake as he seems?"

"The lowest creature in this world!" said the girl. "He was even able to put in my father's mind some doubts about me—to make it seem best to my father that I should not come into the money till I was married. That was because Nellihan knew that I loved David Holman, that David was sentenced to death, that if he died I would never marry anyone. Don't you see? And Nellihan was the next heir."

"I understand," said Silver. "And in a short time he would have found a way to put you out of your misery. I have to leave you. Holman is going to live. Don't doubt that. And trust everything to Bench and Kenyon. I know how you feel about Kenyon, but I don't know what else you could have done. You tried to do a small wrong in order to do a great right. But I suppose that sacrificing one man for another is never a good business. However, that thing will be straightened out. Kenyon will do whatever you want. He'll get a divorce in Nevada, I suppose. And afterward I'll find ways in which you and Holman can manage to repay him."

"If you could do that!" cried the girl.

"Don't pity him too much," said Silver. "He's having his great chance to be a man just as Holman had his chance. Holman was remade. Kenyon is being remade, too. If he lives through it, he'll be able to respect him self for the rest of his life. He was simply a good natured, haphazard, ramshackle cow-puncher and stag driver before this."

"And you?" said the girl suddenly. "What will you gain by all that you've done for Ned, for me, for David?"

"I'm having the fun of it," said Silver with a faint laugh. "And the rest of you are having the pain."

She did not try to answer him. He went back to Parade, saddled the horse, and rode him to the side of the wounded man.

"Heads up, Holman?" said he.

"Clear up in the sky," said Holman. "Arizona, I've tried to persuade you not to go near that devil in his own roost in Tuckaway. I know that you're going, any way. But I want to say this last thing: Everything will be harder than you expect to find it!"

"Thanks," said Silver. "If you say that a thing is hard, I know that you mean it. But I've got to go. Holman, adios! We'll be together in a luckier time."

He turned Parade, and the stallion moved down the slope over the edge of the mountain shoulder. He went carefully, for the voice of his master was hushing him, and Parade glided through the brush like a hunting cat, making never a sound.

Chapter XXII

WAYLAND'S PLACE

THE house of "Buster" Wayland had formerly been the house of the leading banker of the little town of Tuckaway. Simonson had taken an entire block, planted an evergreen hedge around the outside of it, and a grove of trees inside. Within the trees he had established a lawn, and within the lawn stood the house and the stables. The house itself was a frame dwelling, square, plain, and dignified, because Simonson had taste as good as it was simple.

Silver rode his horse right in through the big open gate, but turned aside from the driveway into a dark cloud of trees close to the lawn. There he dismounted and spent a few moments patting Parade and giving him those whispering injunctions which would make him stand fast until his master's whistle summoned him, or his master's voice.

In the meantime, Silver himself was taking breath, and clearing his wits, as it were, by deep breathing. He was still dressed, of course, in the ragged, stained white clothes which he had worn before. And therefore no eye could fall on him without suspicion. He would have to move invisible to the very moment when he began action. And even what that action was to be, he had very little idea. He was like an actor who walks out before the curtain to entertain a crowd, and who must improvise his speeches on the spur of the moment.

He left the horse at last and made a circle of the house. All along the front and rear and one side it was lighted. On the fourth side there was not a light showing.

The ground windows were low, and the first one that Silver looked through showed him the dining room with Buster Wayland and three guests at the table, and a Chinaman, humpbacked with anxious effort, gliding about to serve them.

It was not hard to guess that the man at the head of the table was Wayland. All of his nickname of "Buster" showed in his big, florid face, in the sheen of his eyes, in his continual smiling or laughter. He was big. He was so big that he overflowed his armchair. His gestures and his voice were of the overflowing type, also, and as Silver looked at him, he could not help having a flash back at the wounded man who lay on the shoulder of the mountain with only the vaguest of hopes of giving him comfort.

As for the guests, they were men worth seeing. One of them was none other than Sheriff Bert Philips, whom Silver had last seen in the town of Mustang. The other two, it came instantly to knowledge, were deputies who were assisting Philips in the man hunt. They were talking of that, and of nothing else, and the banker was assuring the sheriff that there would be an adequate reward paid outside of the promise of the law once young Holman was accounted for.

"How he's kept away this long, nobody can make out!" declared Buster Wayland. He bumped the table with his fist. "But it's a certain sure thing he can't keep away much longer."

"It's nothing but Jim Silver, or Silvertip, or whatever you want to call him." declared the sheriff. "He's the fellow who has saved the scalp of Holman. And to think that I had him under my gun in Mustang, and didn't shoot."

"Aye, that was a mistake," growled the raw-boned young deputy whose fierce eyes faced Silver from the opposite side of the table.

"A mistake," agreed Wayland. "But I know how it is—a man wants to give the other fellow every chance unless you're dead sure!"

"There's Silver's record, besides," said the sheriff

'He's been at outs with the law before this, but he always turns up right and the law turns up wrong. He proves his case, and it ain't always the law's case."

"One day he'll wake up dead before his proving is finished," said the deputy with the burning eyes.

"But there's money behind that crowd," said Wayland. "Silver, as you call him, may be honest most of the time, but that girl has money enough to bribe a saint."

"Maybe so—maybe so," said the sheriff. "But what counts with me is that Holman is still on the loose in the mountains."

"We'll hunt him out of there," said the second deputy, an older and a graver man, with a thick red neck and a bristling mustache.

"I think," said Bert Philips, "that maybe we'll do a good job if we simply keep a lot of men riding on the lookout down in the plains, not so far from Tuckaway. Remember that Ned Kenyon is with 'em, and Kenyon knows the lay of the land around here pretty good."

The truth of this remark pinched the memory of Silvertip. Whatever happened, he must get back to the party in time to warn them that Kenyon's suggestion would simply lead them into ruin. They must keep back among the mountains.

"If they're in the mountains," said Buster Wayland, "they'll soon come out on the run. That fellow Nelthan that came in and talked with me to-day, he's as keen as mustard, and he knows his business. He took all the best horses and the best riders out of this town when he scooted back for the hills. He'll work all night, if there's starlight enough to show him the difference between a rock and a bush."

"We'll get 'em," agreed the sheriff. "But only because Holman is wounded. It's a good thing that Lorens shot straight that time. Because if Silver's hands weren't tied down by the moving of a wounded man, I don't think that we'd ever see hide or hair of that party."

The second deputy put in: "What I wanta know is

this—who had the nerve to tell the lie that a horse ever
walked across the bridge in Whistling Canyon? I know
that bridge. I've been across it, and it's made me sick
at the stomach to go over. I've ridden twenty miles out
of my way to keep from having to cross that bridge.
And now some blockheads tell me that a big stallion
up and crossed it—this fellow Silver's horse!"

"Aye, but that horse is Parade," said the sheriff.
"You can't judge him by ordinary horses any more
than you can judge Silver by ordinary men."

"How come?" asked Wayland.

"Parade was the hundred-thousand-dollar mustang
that used to run wild up there in the Sierra Blanca
Desert. Never hear of that?"

"Sure I have!" agreed Wayland.

"That's the one. Seventeen hands of thunder and
lightning, and all gold and twenty-four carats. That's
Parade. They say he'll stand up and cakewalk when his
master whistles. And it's a sure thing that he *did* walk
that bridge, because he wasn't left on the near side
with the other mustang."

"We'll have a drink," said Wayland. "Hey, Sammy,
bring in another bottle of that rye. We're going to have
a drink to the lucky man that crashes a slug of lead
through the brain of that scoundrel of a thief, that
David Holman. The man that has that luck is going to
collect an extra two thousand dollars from me, and
you're all my witnesses!"

They looked at one another, and Silver gritted his
teeth. To cow-punchers who worked for forty-five dollars a month, two thousand meant a huge fortune. Almost anything would be done for the sake of that
money. Now it was stacked on top of the original five
thousand that had been hung up as a prize, and nothing could save David Holman—nothing but some way
of proving his innocence.

Silver kicked off his sandals. Even their light weight
would be in his way now.

He rounded to the front of the house, shinnied up
one of the wooden columns that framed the Georgian

porch, and so came to the second story of the big house. A balcony ran down the side of the building, and he could move at ease down this.

There were only two lighted rooms, one a big bedroom, and one an upstairs study with a big easy-chair in front of a fireplace, and a silk dressing gown and a pair of slippers laid out. Mr. Buster Wayland would probably take his ease here after dinner had been finished.

But the furnishings of the room did not end here—here was also a big steel safe in a corner of the room. It was hardly a decorative piece, but it had more interest for the owner of the house, no doubt, than all the rest of the place that Simonson had built.

The safe was not all. There was also an element of human interest, for in a corner of the room, seated beside the only lighted lamp in the chamber, was a guard.

Holman had said that Wayland knew how to attach things to his interest, and certainly this fellow was a perfect example and type of ruffian. He was reading a magazine with such interest that his brutal head was thrust far forward on his neck, and his face snarled with the emotions that worked in him.

Something that Silver did not hear in the least reached the ear of the fellow. Instantly he was out of the chair, crouching, a gun in his hand. He went cat-like to the door, opened it, and then came slowly back, his mouth still working, his eyes glaring.

He was not a man. He was simply a formidable beast. Once back in his chair, he remained for a time alert, in a singular way, reading, or pretending to read, and suddenly flashing his glance up and around the room.

Then the truth was borne in upon Silver. It was the gaze that he himself kept fastened on the gunman that made the fellow uneasy, the insistent force of that regard constantly bearing in upon his unconscious mind, and vaguely sending messages of warning to the consciousness itself.

The man wriggled and stirred as though he were seated too close to a hot fire. Never had Silver seen instinct work more powerfully and on so slight a cause.

Presently the man sprang out of the chair and walked straight across the room and to the window where Silver was watching. Silver flattened himself close to the wall of the house, raising in his right hand a revolver which he grasped by the barrel, the butt offering as the club.

And after a moment a bullethead came out through the window, not slowly, but with a quick, dripping motion so fast that the blow that Silvertip aimed at the base of the man's neck found the very top of his head instead.

The weight of that shock drove his face down against the sill, but did not quite stun him. Silver, following his attack with wonderful speed, saw his man on one knee before the window, with a gun coming gradually into his hand. There was no need for another blow. Silver simply tapped him across the forehead and the gun slid to the rug.

The whole soul of the guard was striving to fight, but the numbed body and brain could not react. The face of the man was a frightful thing to see. It was like the twisted mask of an ape trying to bite.

He kept shaking his head to clear away the clouds that were gathering over his wits. Silver tied the vaguely struggling hands of the man behind his back before sense enough to cry out came to the thug. He tilted back his head, and his chest heaved before he let out the yell.

It was never uttered. Silver simply stepped in front of him and put the muzzle of the Colt into that open mouth. The apelike creature clamped his teeth down on the steel and gasped.

Silver removed the gun and looked over his captive.

"What's your name, brother?" he asked. "And talk soft when you answer."

"What the devil is my name to you?" snarled the

captive. "What I'm goin' to do to a sneakin' slick of a second-story worker like you when I get my chance—"

He paused, as though realizing the futility of threats at this moment. His breath came straining and rasping in his throat. The butt of the gun had cut his scalp a little, and a crimson trickle, having worked through the hair, spilled down beside his right eye, and gradually worked in a crooked course toward the chin.

"What's your name?" repeated Silver.

"Lefty some call me, and Soggy some call me," said the yegg.

"All right, Soggy," said Silver. "That name goes for me. Tell me when Mr. Wayland comes up to this room?"

"Why should I tell you?"

"Because he's going to be wiped out of this town, Soggy," said Silver. "He may be wiped off the face of the earth. I don't know. The fact is that if I have to drop him, your own name will be mud around this neck of the woods. Am I wrong?"

"Soggy" said nothing. He merely lowered his head a little and glowered at Silver from beneath shaggy brows.

"It would be hard to explain," said Silver. "Wayland is a big man in this town. If anything happens to him, it might be tough on his hired gunman. Lynching parties work pretty fast around here."

Soggy pursed out his lips in thought. He said nothing.

"I'm going to tie you into that chair," said Silver. "If I have to, I'll choke you with a gag, but I'd rather give you a chance to breathe comfortably. Walk over there and sit down. Remember, I'm giving you a better break than you'd give me. And if you try to yell, I may have to sink a chunk of lead in you."

Chapter XXIII

A FORCED CONFESSION

Soggy, without a word of protest, let himself be tied into the chair. And Silver even made a cigarette, lighted it, and put it between the lips of his captive. Thereafter, by ducking his head far down, Soggy could manage to transfer the cigarette from his mouth to his right hand, which was tied out on the arm of the chair in which he sat. Silver stood back and grinned at him, and Soggy grinned back.

"Hard lines!" sympathized Silver.

"I've seen worse," said Soggy. "I've seen worse birds than you are, too. What's your monicker?"

"I work with quite a batch of 'em," said Silver.

"I'll bet you do," agreed Soggy.

"Arizona Jim, some call me."

"Arizona," said Soggy, "you're kind of white. What's the game on Wayland?"

"He's a thug and a crook," said Silver. "He has a lot coming to him, and he's going to get part of it, or all of it, to-night."

"I like to hear you, kind of," said Soggy. "The while I been workin' for him ain't been so sweet. Easy money—but he's a bum. He's a four-flusher."

"He can fight," said Silver tentatively.

"That's what *he* says," answered Soggy. He added: "If you hand him the rap, do you give me a break to get loose out of here?"

"If you don't bother me," said Silver.

"I'll sit like a bird in a tree," said Soggy. "Go ahead and blaze away, will you?"

"I'll go ahead, and I'll blaze away," agreed Silver. "Know anything good about this fellow Wayland?"

"No. Nothin'."

"Don't even know when he'll come up here?"

"No. Maybe in an hour. Maybe any time. He comes up here off and on to see how things go. He's got his heart and his liver and his lights locked up in the safe yonder. Some mug that cracks that safe open will get a hand-out worth havin'! And if—"

Silver raised a hand for silence. He heard something on the stairs beyond the room. He heard a rhythmic thing—a pressure rather than a sound—coming down the hall toward the door. Stepping close to the door, flattening his body against the wall, he saw the door suddenly swing open. Big Wayland, with a step surprisingly light and fast for a man of his size, strode into the room.

His first glance was for the face of the safe. But while he was taking it, he saw his gunman tied into the chair, and the ominous gun in the hand of Silver, just beside him.

There was good fighting stuff in Wayland, after all. With his right hand he reached for his gun. With his left he drove a long, straight, whipping punch at the head of Silver. The latter let the blow go past him. He stepped in and jabbed the muzzle of his Colt into the ribs of Wayland. With his left he caught the gun hand of the big fellow.

So for an instant they faced one another, Wayland glaring, the eyes of Silver utterly cold and remorseless. The thumb of his right hand was trembling with desire to let the hammer drop and ease this crooked life out of the world.

Wayland saw the expression and seemed to understand it. He said in a low, guttural voice: "All right. You've got me. Who are you? What do you want?"

"They've been talking about me down at your table," said Silver. "They call me Silver, or Silvertip, but names don't make much difference. This is a business call, Wayland. Give me that gun!"

He took the gun. It was the only weapon the banker carried, as Silver discovered by sliding his hand rapidly over the body of the man.

When he was disarmed, Silver stepped back from him and said calmly:

"You don't need to hoist your hands over your head. Just remember that I'm watching you, Wayland. Now take a sheet of that paper, sit down at the table, unscrew your fountain pen, and write a little letter for me."

"What sort? A letter of credit? Is that what you're driving at?" asked Wayland.

"A letter to whomever it concerns," said Silver. "Saying that you hired the two crooks who took young Holman down to the bank, that you went with them, that you helped yourself to one third of the loot, that when you saved the bank afterward, you were simply using money that you'd already stolen from it for that purpose, and for buying out poor Simonson before he died of a broken heart. Is that clear?"

Wayland showed not the least surprise.

"Write a little story that clears young Mr. Holman. Is that it?" he asked.

Then he turned toward the tied-up gunman.

"You let yourself be brushed out of the picture, did you, Soggy?"

"He socked me," said Soggy. "But I dunno that I'm sorry, if I'm goin' to have a chance to see him sock you, too!"

"You can't go through with this," said Wayland to Silver. "I have men down there waiting for me. They'll be up to see what's wrong if I stay here. Besides, you're only making a fool of yourself. You're going to force a confession out of me, and a forced confession isn't worth anything, and I've got Soggy here as a witness to the force used. Look here, Silver, you're a fellow with a bright eye. You're the sort of a man who ought to be able to tell on which side your bread is buttered. And I'm an open-handed fellow, Silver, if people approach me in the right way. You could have a fair—"

He stopped. Something in the face of Silver told him he was wasting time—a cold and profound disgust.

"Sit down," said Silver, "and write. Begin with the date line, and go down to the finish. Understand? I know what the form should be, and so do you. Now write!"

The big man sat at the table, his face shining with sweat, the fatness of the fountain pen looking actually slender in his bulky hand.

"You can't bleed me," he gasped finally. "You can't do anything with a forced confession. I can laugh at this to-morrow."

"You won't be here to-morrow," said Silver.

"Murder?" said Wayland, steadily enough.

"I don't think so—unless you fail to write," said Silver. "To kill you wouldn't be murder, Wayland. But if you write the stuff out, I'm simply going to take you downtown and see you catch the freight that's pulling out of the station in about forty minutes. You'll catch that train, and Soggy will catch it with you. When the confession is found in here and you're found gone, I think it may do something, Wayland. But because I know you'd rather die than tell the truth and lose all your loot at the same time, I'm going to give you another sort of a chance with that. I'm going to let you open that safe and take what's in it along with you."

"To become a fugitive of justice, eh?" said Wayland, narrowing his eyes.

"You've been that before, or my eye can't read straight," said Silver. "Start writing!"

One desperate glance Wayland flung around the room. Then he compressed his lips and began to write. The room fell utterly silent, so silent that the scratching of the pen seemed to be growing louder and louder, and Silver became aware of the ticking of the big clock that stood on the mantelpiece above the chimney place.

He was aware of something else, too, after a time,

and that was the approach of footfalls up the stairs. Big Wayland stopped writing, and his face lighted.

"If it's one of your guests," said Silver, turning the key in the door, "tell him that you're busy. That you'll be right down. Understand?"

Wayland nodded. But a fugitive hope was glimmering in his eyes all the time.

Presently a hand beat on the door firmly.

"Hello?" called Wayland, looking straight into the muzzle of Silver's gun.

"Hello, Wayland. This is Bert Philips. Wondered what was keeping you."

"Coming down in a minute," said Wayland. But there was a shaking huskiness in his voice that made Philips exclaim:

"Wayland! I want to see you, man!"

He rattled the knob of the door. He had found enough in the absence of his host, he had heard enough in the voice of that host, to alarm him. There was no doubt about it. Wayland would have to admit him; at least, see him face to face.

"You've been upset," whispered Silver to Wayland. "Tell him that. Go unlock the door and face him—but if you let him come into the room, I start shooting, and I shoot at you. You hear?"

Wayland rolled despairing eyes. Then he nodded, went to the door and turned the key. The door came instantly open, as though Philips were pushing against it. But Wayland held it by the knob, and the sheriff was saying:

"I'm worried about you, man. And you look green-gray. You're sweating. What the devil's the matter? May I come in?"

"I've been upset a little, is all. A little sick," muttered Wayland. "You go back and keep the boys entertained. I'll be down in a little while. Don't worry, I'm all right. Just keep the boys entertained for a bit, will you?"

"Well," said Philips uneasily, "well, I'll do that. But I'm worried about you. Sure that nothing's wrong?"

"No," said Wayland. "I'm all right!"

What torment it must have been for him to speak those words!

But they were spoken, the door closed against Philips, and the lock softly turned back.

Tottering in his step, his head hanging, Wayland went back to the table. Suddenly he said:

"Silver, I'll make you rich! I'll pay you—"

"Listen," said Silver sternly. "If you had ten millions in gold and you could give it to me with a wave of the hand, I'd still laugh at you!"

For one moment Wayland stared at that grim face. Then he resumed his writing.

As he finished it, Silver, looking over his shoulder, read the document, and knew as the signature went down that the thing was perfect. If anything could save Holman, this was it—if only Wayland could be removed, so that it would look as though conscience had forced a confession from him before he fled with a part of his loot.

He pushed the paper onto the center of the table, favored Silver with a scowl of the blackest hate, and then hurried to the safe. The combination wheel spun back and forth for an instant under his fat fingers. The heavy door opened with a faint puffing sound, and there was Wayland on his knees, at work.

He knew where every item of the highest value was to be found. Perhaps, crook that he was, he had the cream of his wealth collected there against just such an emergency as this. At any rate, in five minutes he was on his feet again, with his pockets stuffed. Silver, stepping to the side of Soggy, with a touch of the knife had made the thug free, merely whispering:

"Soggy, you're going to climb on board the same train with him. You know where the pies are. Maybe you'll be able to help yourself to some of 'em."

Soggy rolled up his face with a frightful grin distorting it, and a flare of the big, apish nostrils. Suddenly Silver knew that he could trust the man to work honestly with him during the rest of that adventure.

And he was right. He had no fear of the gun that he entrusted to Soggy. It was simply another proof that Wayland would not be able to get away. His figure was definitely settled.

They passed out along the balcony. Soggy went to the ground first. Wayland then with stifled grunts of effort followed, to slide down the pillar at the end of the porch, while Silver hung by his hands from the edge of the balcony above and then dropped lightly to the ground. That was how the trio reassembled, and started across the grounds. The thinnest sort of a whistle summoned Parade out of the trees to the side of his master, and now Silver walked behind the pair, occasionally spurring big Wayland forward with a word.

No one noticed the leading citizen of Tuckaway as he strode down alleys and across the little town toward the railroad station, or as he went under the guidance of Silver a little distance down the tracks to a point where a rising grade made it certain that the next freight could be boarded.

It was not until the train came groaning and thundering near, however, that Wayland realized a new feature of danger in his plight.

"You've given Soggy a gun!" he exclaimed. "It's the same as murder for me to get on board the train with him. He'll bump me off as sure as daylight! He's bound to!"

"I've got a spare gun for you, too," said Silver. "You can have it as soon as the headlight of the engine goes by."

"Hold on!" yelled Soggy. "Don't I get any edge on that big thug after I've—"

But the approaching thunder of the train drowned his voice. The headlight of the engine went by, printed the swinging shadows of the leaves of the bushes on the faces of the three men.

It was now that Silver put a Colt into the hand of Wayland.

"Now hop that train!" he shouted. "Because if

you're still here after it goes by, you shoot it out with me!"

Then, kneeling at a gap in the brush, Silver, with poised gun, watched Wayland rush for the train. He saw Soggy leap like a monkey and catch with hands and feet. He saw big Wayland catch one of the iron ladders with almost equal agility. And then the train swayed on and passed out of view around the next turn, gathering speed all the while.

It was already shooting along with a speed which would break the neck of any man who tried to leap from it. And many and many a mile would be between Wayland and the town of Tuckaway before he could start the return journey. Day would have come again, and the news of his disappearance and of his confession, before he could get back. And with the news, there would be a run on the bank unless the directors of it closed the doors.

All the consequences were obscured before the eyes of Silver, except he knew that he had kept himself from shooting a rascal who needed killing—and that he had assured the safe return of David Holman to the ranks of the law-abiding citizens.

Chapter XXIV

KENYON'S SACRIFICE

HE had assured the return of Holman—if only he could bring help to his friends in the mountains before the cruel wits of Nellihan and Lorens had located the wounded man and his companions.

Silver drove Parade like a golden streak straight back for the house of Wayland. He checked the stallion in front of the porch. Inside the house, he could hear a heavy battering at a door. Were they at last sufficiently alarmed to beat down the door?

He rapped on the front door, in his turn. The Chinaman opened it before him, and then winced back at the sight of the tall body and the white rags it was dressed in.

"Is the sheriff here?" asked Silver. "Then go tell him that Jim Silver is down here waiting to see him."

The Chinaman fled up the stairs, his hands outstretched to help him, like wings, his head jerking over a shoulder, now and then, to cast furtive glances back at the big man who waited in the hall.

Upstairs, the battering paused for an instant, and Silver heard the voice of one of the deputies exclaim: "Mr. Wayland, if you don't open the door, we'll take for granted that something has happened to you, and we're going to break it down!"

The voice of the Chinaman broke in on this. There was a sudden exclamation from the sheriff, then the stamp of his running feet on the hall floor above.

Silver sang out: "I'm down here, Philips, and I'm not fighting."

Yet the first thing that he saw come down the

dimness of the stairs was the glimmer of a revolver,
and then the dark outlines of Philips crouched behind
the gun.

Silver put his hands up, shoulder high.

"I'm not fighting," he said. "Tell me if you know
that Wayland has run out of town with all the cash he
could get together. And then come down here and
pinch me, if you want to!"

"Break down that door, Gene!" called the sheriff to
one of the deputies.

Then he came hurrying down and confronted Silver.

"Silver," he said, "keep those hands up till I've
fanned you. You know you're wanted for knowingly
and willingly and witting—or whatever the legal
phrases are—helping that rat of a Dave Holman to escape!"

"Fan me, Bert," said Silver. "There's a gun under
the pit of my left arm, and there's a knife on my left
hip. Take 'em both!"

The door went down with a crash while he was
speaking. Philips took him into the dining room, where
the Chinaman remained quaking in a corner.

"It's the queerest layout that I've ever seen," declared Philips. "I've never known anything like it. I
hope I never *do* know anything like it. Wayland has
turned into a green-faced mystery. You say that he's
gone out of town and—"

There was a loud shouting from above, and then the
thundering of heavy feet on the stairs. The first deputy,
he of the fierce eyes, rushed into the room, with the
signed confession of Wayland fluttering like a white
flag in his hand.

He slapped it onto the table in front of Philips and
cried: "Bert we been ridin' all this way for nothin'. The
scalp of this here gent, this David Holman, it ain't
worth a damaged nickel—because the whole yarn
about him robbing the bank was a lie. Here's the
truth!"

The sheriff was not a slow-minded man, but when
he had finished reading that paper for the third time,

he said: "But what persuaded Wayland to confess? If he's been this much of a skunk, why should he ever have confessed?"

The deputy pointed at Silver.

"Him!" he said. He must've done it!"

"We want Wayland, not Holman," said the sheriff "Where did you say that Wayland is?"

"On a freight train bound east. You can telegraph ahead, but I don't think he'll arrive at the first station," said Silver.

"Why not?" asked Philips.

"Because he may have some trouble on the road," answered Silver. "Philips, if you don't want Holman you don't want me."

"I don't want you," agreed Philips. "I might have known that you'd prove the law wrong, again! Poor Holman! Something ought to be done to make up to him what he's gone through!"

Silver had lowered his hands, slowly, while Gene watched him with starved, bright eyes, as though he hated to see this quarry slip through his hands.

"The great thing you can do," said Silver, "is to see that the men of Kirby Crossing don't mob Holman and the others during the night. Nellihan and Lorens are leading those men from Kirby, and you can bet your money that they'll keep moving all night. Philips, will you get on your horse and make a drive toward Kenda Mountain, yonder? That's where I left Holman and the other three—up on a shoulder."

"I know the place," said the sheriff. "I'll get there as fast as horseflesh is able to fetch me. I'll be with you in two minutes, as soon as we can saddle up."

Silver stepped to the window, and sent a whistle cutting into the outer night.

"I'm going on ahead," he said. "Parade will take me there ahead of you. There's enough moonlight for straight shooting, and I'm worried about what may be happening up there. So long! You know the place Ride your horses to a finish!"

Hoofbeats sounded softly on the lawn, and came

a sliding halt on the gravel of the path beside the house. The sheriff saw the sheen of the golden stallion in the lamplight. Then Silver was through the window and into the saddle. He was gone in a flash into the night.

It was almost at that moment that on the shoulder of Kendal Mountain, Harry Bench laid his hand on his sleeping companion, Ned Kenyon. As Kenyon wakened, he heard Bench saying:

"They're coming, Ned! Get up and out of here, fast! They're not fifty steps away. Listen!"

Kenyon heard a soft crackling, as a twig snapped. He was up instantly, sweeping his blanket into a roll.

He saw, then, that the girl had not slept. She sat passively beside Holman. He had thrown out his hand, during his sleep, and she held it in both of hers. One gesture from Bench told her of the danger. She sprang up. Holman wakened with a start. In a moment Bench and Kenyon were carrying their wounded companion on the litter away from the little clearing.

The moon was less than half full, but it shed a light that seemed to be growing stronger and stronger, as though danger were brightening it. If those who hunted for them found the place where they had camped, might not they also be able to find the out trail they were following?

Kenyon carried the head of the litter and led the way. They went down the first slope until it entered the head of a ravine that wound on through the foothills, growing deeper every moment.

"This here—it's a trap!" said Harry Bench. "Suppose that they come down on us here, they'll just flood us away!"

"If we kept up there on the divides," said Kenyon, "they could see us miles away, under this moon. We ain't in this valley because we like it, but because there ain't any better place for us to go!"

That was the sheer truth. They went on silently and had put a good mile behind them when a gun spoke from the cliff at their right.

No bullet came near them. Three times the rifle wa
fired in rapid succession, and looking up, thei
frightened eyes saw a horseman wheeling his mustan
away from the edge of the cliff, and going out of sigh
at a dead gallop. His wild Indian yell came whoopin
dimly down to them.

The men of Kirby Crossing had found them. The
could guess that, and it would not be long before th
flood of fighters came sweeping down into the ravine
as fast as horseflesh could carry them. They put dow
the litter and stared at one another.

Holman said: "It's all right, boys. You've done mor
than any other men in the world could have done. Th
luck's against us, at last, and that's all. I can take th
medicine. Stand back and hoist your hands if they sigh
you. Or better still, try to climb out of the canyon an
get away. They may rough you up a little if they fin
you with me; but if you're not in sight, they'll be gla
enough to get me, and they're not likely to keep o
hunting for you."

The girl said nothing. As usual, she merely looked a
Harry Bench, for she was rarely able even to glanc
toward Ned Kenyon.

It was Kenyon who made the answer to that last re
mark, however. He said: "Harry, we're in the narrow
of the canyon. One man oughta be able to hold bac
a crowd for quite a spell, here. And while he's holdin
the other man and Edith can fetch Holman along ti
you come to some cut-back at the side of the ravine—
some place where you can hole up and hide."

He took out a silver dollar, new-minted, flashing i
the moonlight, and laid it on the back of his thumb.

"Call, Harry!" said he, and spun the coin high in
the air.

Harry Bench looked up at the rising of the coin wi
despairing eyes. It was life or death, he knew, that wa
being tossed for. The man who remained behind, a
Kenyon had so calmly suggested, would check th
flood for a time, but it was sure to beat him down an
roll on, before any long time.

"Tails!" called Bench.

The coin spatted on the palm of Kenyon. Bench leaned forward to look at it, but instantly the long fingers of Kenyon furled over it.

"It's tails," said Kenyon. "It's tails, all right. You win, and I stay here."

"I won't stand for it!" groaned Holman. "Go and save yourselves, both of you, and take Edith."

Confusion of mind and doubt bred something like anger in the voice of Harry Bench.

"She won't leave you, you blockhead!" exclaimed Bench. "There ain't any other way about it than this. Heaven help Ned—but the luck was agin him. Edith, pick up the light end of the litter, there."

He himself picked up the head of the litter. But the girl had run to Kenyon.

"Come on with us, Ned!" she said. "If anything happens to you, even if the rest of us lived, would our lives be anything but a curse and a darkness?"

"I ain't going to be killed," said Kenyon. "I feel kind of calm, and lucky. Say 'Good-by' and go fast."

"Come on!" cried Bench, "or I'll start draggin' him by myself!"

He began, in fact, to stride forward, trailing one end of the poles behind him.

"Go on," said Kenyon. "It's what I want you to do!"

Still, for an instant, she hesitated.

"Heaven will never forgive me for what I've done to you! But can *you* forgive me, Ned?" she asked him.

Holman was crying out wildly, ordering Bench to drop the litter, swearing that he would not accept a life given to him in this fashion. Kenyon took the girl by the arm and waved her toward Holman.

"He's a better man than me," said Kenyon. "Go help him. Forgive you? They're ain't anything to forgive. God bless you; good-by!"

She seemed to Kenyon, suddenly, like a child that stared up with incredulous wonder, and awe. What she said, he could not understand, because her voice was

choked. And then she was gone, and Kenyon stood
looking down at the hand which she had kissed.

He saw her pick up the dragging poles of the litter
and so the group disappeared around the corner of the
wall of the ravine, and the protesting voice of Holman
grew faint. At the same time, the clanging hoofs of
many horses came roaring into the upper end of the
valley.

Kenyon looked up at the sky, where the moon made
it pale with light. He looked down at the walls of the
canyon, one black as ink, one shimmering softly with
the moonshine. He felt that he was about to die, and
this picture was in some manner entering his very soul.

There was only one bit of shelter for him—a fallen
boulder that projected two feet or more above the
sand. Behind that he stretched himself and put the rifle
to his shoulder. And then he saw them come pouring—a great sweep of horsemen, darkly silhouetted
against the moonlight wall of the ravine. He fired three
shots and waited.

They were not aimed shots. He was no good with a
rifle. Besides, he had no intention of shooting to kill.
And he drew a great breath of relief when he saw the
cavalcade split away to either side, suddenly, as though
the prow of an invisible ship had cloven a way through
them, pushing them back under the shadows of the
cliffs. He saw one man dismount and begin to climb by
a crevice up the sheer face of the ravine wall. That
would be the end—when that fellow gained the top of
the wall and could shoot down at an easy angle into
the body of the man who blocked the passing of the ravine. But Ned Kenyon did not turn and run for his life.
If there were fear in him, he could not recognize its
presence, but all he felt was a calm happiness that had
no regard whatever for the future.

Chapter XXV

THE SHOW-DOWN

IT took one hour for a horseman to get from Tuckaway to Kendal Mountain. It took forty minutes for Silver to rush out from the town on the back of Parade. As he reached the abandoned camping place, he heard the rifles open in the ravine below. So he swept down from the heights like a hawk from the upper air, and came into the narrow ravine where the guns boomed like small cannon. Then, at an elbow turn of the wall, he had a chance to view the scene in detail, without being looked at himself.

Close under the walls of the ravine, chiefly on the side where the shadow made a black apron, a dozen or fifteen men were taking shelter behind brush, or behind fragments of rock that had fallen from the cliffs above. Their rifles spurted little jets of fire, now and then. In answer to them there was an occasional shot from a point where the canyon narrowed until the wall of it seemed to be leaning together. Those solitary shots were fired by big Harry Bench and Kenyon, of course, and beyond the narrows of the ravine would be the wounded Dave Holman, and the girl.

Now Silver saw the greatest threatening danger—the small silhouette of a man who was climbing the eastern wall of the ravine, working himself up on the jags of a deep crevice. In a few moments, the fellow would be on the upper lip of the canyon cliff, and could destroy the defenders with ease and security.

Silver dismounted, and pressing close to the corner of the rock so that little of his body would show, he made his voice great and thundered:

169

"Kirby Crossing! Who's there to talk to Jim Silver? I've got news from Tuckaway. The sheriff's on the run to get out here. Buster Wayland has confessed he did the job of robbing the bank. Holman has clean hands. He's cleared."

There was a chorus of surprised shouts, and then a yell in which he recognized the snarling, high-pitched voice of Nellihan:

"He lies! It's a bluff! Why isn't the sheriff here before him? Boys, stand tight. We'll bag the whole lot of them in another minute. Lorens is on top, and we've got the lot of them!"

A yell of triumph ran in on the last of his words, for now the man who climbed the eastern wall had reached the top, and was running forward to gain a better position from which to shoot down into the ravine. That savage yell told Silver that he had come too late to use words. Only his rifle would help him now, and whipping it out of the saddle holster, he lay flat and drew a careful bead. First he ranged his eye down the side of the ravine to estimate the range, then he caught the dark silhouette of the target in his sights, and began to squeeze his hand over the trigger.

At that moment, Lorens disappeared behind some upjutting rock on the verge of the cliff.

Sweat streamed down the face of Silver. But what could he do? If he rushed with Parade, he might escape the gantlet of fire on either side of the ravine, but when he reached his friends in the narrows, he would simply be swallowed in the same trap that held them.

A moment later, the ravine was hushed, and immediately after that, he heard the clang of a rifle, fired from the top of the cliff. That shot had told, for Lorens, in excess of triumph, suddenly leaped to his feet with a yell that rang from far off, coming to the ears of Silver like the cry of a bird of prey from the central sky. It was a fatal mistake for Lorens. In rising to brandish his rifle so that it flashed in the moonlight, a meager, whirling streak of brilliance, he had jumped right into the sights of Silver's gun.

Nellihan's howling voice shrilled a warning, but it was heard too late. Silver fired. And the body of Lorens leaned slowly out. The rifle dropped before him. Then he shot out into the air in a graceful arc, like a high diver, and plunged from the height.

A great yell of rage and of horror came from the men of Kirby Crossing. Before it died out, Silver was in the saddle again and sending Parade down the ravine like a glimmering bolt of lightning.

The watchers were taken totally by surprise. A few turned their guns on him, but the shots they fired were random bullets, before he plunged into the shadows of the narrows. And as he went by, he saw the body of poor Ned Kenyon, spread-eagled behind the rock.

Dead?

He ranged Parade close against the canyon wall beyond the reach of the bullets; then he ran forward, stooping low, and gained the side of Kenyon. A faint muttering sound came from the lips of his friend. He turned the limp body, and saw a patch of darkness high on the breast of Kenyon, a patch that grew.

"Arizona?" said Ned Kenyon faintly. "I might 'a' known that you'd get in on the thing before the wind-up. Have they blotted me?"

Silver thumbed the wound. The bullet had entered high on the shoulder, close to the base of the back of the neck; it had ranged forward and come out by the collar bone.

"Take one deep breath—and say one word!" said Silver.

Kenyon obediently breathed and said: "Damn!" clipping his teeth together as he spoke.

Silver sighed with relief. "If that bullet had got the lungs," he said, "there'd be bubbles of blood in your mouth when you talk. Ned, if I can get you out of this trap, you'll live! Try to lift your left arm. No? It's broken, then; the collar bone's broken, at least. But that's nothing. Where are the others?"

He had an answer from behind for that. They heard the crunching of a heavy footfall, and the great bulk of

One-eyed Harry cast itself down beside them. He gasped:

"Thank Heaven you're here, Jim. I came back as soon as I got the girl and Holman stowed away in a little canyon that rips back from this here, a short ways down. Holman is raisin' the devil, and tryin' to break away and crawl back here, so's he can die with the rest of us; and the girl's praying for you out loud, Kenyon; and Holman says he never was worth one of your old boots. Who's that out there, looking at the moon?"

For not far in front of the rock there was the body of Lorens, stretched on its back and staring steadily up at the moon, which glinted on the dead eyes.

There was no chance for Silver or Kenyon to answer the question, for the voice of Nellihan, raised to an animal howl, was now urging the men of Kirby Crossing to close in and rush the defenders. And a great, bull voice made answer:

"Where's yourself, Nellihan? Close in and lead up, instead of talkin' from the back row of the church!"

"I'm here!" shouted Nellihan. "Boys, all together, now. Keep shooting as we go in on 'em. And then—"

"Wait a minute!" called Silver. "All you fellows from Kirby Crossing—if you rush us, we've got three rifles to blow the tar out of a good many of you. If Nellihan wants us, I'll stand out and fight him. If he drops me, you can have the rest of them. They'll surrender. If I drop him, you back up and take a rest till the morning. Does that sound fair to you?"

No one answered for a moment, because there was only one man who could speak, and that was Nellihan. Suddenly his long, misshapen body appeared, striding with long steps from out of the shadows near the wall. He was desperate, as Silver knew, for on this night he was playing his last cards to ruin the life of a girl and get his hands on the fortune.

"I'm here," said Nellihan. "Where are you? Stand out here and show us your face. Are you yellow?"

Silver rose and stood out before the eyes of all those enemies. His hands were empty, and so were the hands of Nellihan, who walked straight up to him and glared into his eyes with a hellish malice.

"You've spoiled everything for me. You've smashed every plan, and you've killed Lorens. You won't hang for that, because I guess he's wanted for more than one killing. But you wouldn't have a chance to hang, anyway. Because I'm going to split your wishbone for you to-night, my friend! Are you ready to start?"

Silver looked at him with a shrinking of the flesh. The man seemed neither old nor young. He was a thing of poisonous evil.

"I'm ready," said Silver. "We'll stand back to back, if you want, and walk away till somebody sings out to shoot. Does that suit you, Nellihan?"

Nellihan peered into his face, as though trying to find the source of the mysterious strength that sustained this man in the time of danger.

"Anything suits me," he said. "You're as good as a dead man, right now. Hey, Baldy! Sing out when you think we've walked far enough!"

They stood back to back. Silver, glancing down, saw that his shadow was sloping well out before him. That meant that when he turned, the moon would be in his eyes. But that was a small disadvantage—if only he could subdue the sick shuddering of his flesh, as he thought of this half-human animal, who would soon be whipping a gun from under his coat and turning to fire. To fight men, Silver felt himself capable; but it was impossible to think of Nellihan failing. The devil he served would support him.

"Start!" shouted the voice of "Baldy."

The murmuring of many other voices died down like a wind passing out of trees. Slowly Silver stepped away, straining every nerve to an electric tension.

"Shoot!" screeched the voice of Baldy.

Silver whirled, snatching his gun from beneath his arm. He saw Nellihan drawing a revolver and leaping far to the side at the same instant. Fast as Silver was, that snaky hand had been faster still. The gun in Nellihan's grip exploded. The brief breath of the bullet fanned the face of Silver as he fired in turn, with his gun hardly more than hip-high.

He thought he had missed, and that Nellihan had deliberately fired a bullet into the ground, for his second shot. It seemed almost—as he held his fire, with his man covered—that Nellihan was slowly dropping on one knee to take a more careful aim. But when he had come to one knee, his body continued to collapse, until he lay face down on the ground.

Death had simply laid its numbing hand upon him gradually.

And before this horror ended, or the silence after it had ceased, the ravine was echoing with the beat of the hoofs of horses. Out from the shadows at the upper end of the valley came three riders, and he who galloped in the lead was Sheriff Bert Philips, bringing up the authentic hand of the law, at last.

All was not as simple as Silver had hoped and even expected. It had looked easy enough on that night, when the men of Kirby Crossing gave up the prey that had baffled them so long, and even helped to take care of the two wounded men. There was no trouble afterward about Nellihan or Lorens, either. Because it was clear that Silver had represented law against mob violence. Furthermore, against Lorens, it was discovered, that there were many counts; and when the character of Nellihan was exposed, the world looked on his death as deliverance from a plague.

Ned Kenyon, too, had a simple rôle. When he was well enough to ride, he went into Nevada to get the divorce that was necessary, and he went without any soreness of the heart. He said to Silver:

"The misery just kind of leaked out of me with my blood, after Lorens had sent the slug through me!"

"You're going to be sensible, I hope," said Silver. "You'll take the help that she and Holman want to give you?"

"Well," said Kenyon, "now that I've got over bein' foolish about her, I guess there's something in what she says—that I worked enough to deserve some pay. So

I'm goin' to take the coin. She wants to give me a regular cattle king's layout. But I'll stick just to the ten thousand that she wanted to give me in the beginning. Small things are better for small men, Jim, and I never was as big as my inches."

All of these matters went very well, but it was a full six months before Holman was able to shake off the hand of the law. Not that any one doubted his story, now, but there were complications which might never have been solved, had it not been that the governor of the State stepped in to cut all the red tape with a complete pardon.

But Silver was far away in the northland when this happened, and he only heard of it through a letter that had followed him from one forwarding address to another.

It was from David Holman, and he said in part:

We've put our heads together, but we don't know what to do. We've owed our happiness to three people—one part to One-eyed Harry Bench, and nine parts to Ned Kenyon, and ninety parts to you. Edith has been able to content Harry and Ned. But we are sorry we can't offer you hard cash, or even a ranch. If we could think of anything you need, we'd like to offer it. But a horse and a gun seem to make you a complete man. All that we can give you is gratitude.

Now that I'm free, and the divorce has been granted, we're going to be married quietly and go for a long trip. When we come back, we'll hope that one day you'll drop in on us. And stay the rest of your life, if you find the place comfortable. The best of all, would be to have you at the wedding. You saw Edith at a wedding once before. That was a marriage in the dark. We hope that this one will be in the sun, with not even a shadow on its future, no matter how much wretchedness may be in its past.

When you write to us, if you ever will, we wish that you could tell us where you are riding. Or do you know yourself, but simply drift with the wind or let Parade follow his fancy?

It was a cold day, and as Silver read that letter in the little post office and then crumpled the paper, he echoed that last question in his own mind. Where was he bound? He could not tell. The ancient melancholy descended upon him, and he fell into long reflections from which he awakened, suddenly, remembering that he had left Parade shivering in the street.